A minute later, I was walking along a wooded mountain path, brushing easily past the branches of wind-twisted trees. I knew, in the way you always know things in dreams, that I was in Montana, exploring.

Behind me, leaves rustled. I turned in time to see something disappearing into the undergrowth. I took a few steps forward. Yellow eyes gleamed at me from the bushes.

Suddenly, I was very afraid. I started to run and, as I ran, I could hear something behind me, but I didn't want to look back.

The path ended abruptly at the edge of a cliff. I wobbled at the brink, catching a dizzying glimpse of rocks and water far below before turning and looking back. I had to see what had been chasing me.

There was nothing there.

And then I fell.

POISON APPLE BOOKS

MIDNIGHT HOWL

by Clare Hutton

POISON APPLE

SCHOLASTIC INC.

New York Toronto London Auckland
Sydney Mexico City New Delhi Hong Kong

For James and Fiona,
who are sometimes wild animals

No part of this publication may be
reproduced, stored in a retrieval system,
or transmitted in any form or by any means,
electronic, mechanical, photocopying, recording,
or otherwise, without written permission of the
publisher. For information regarding permission,
write to Scholastic Inc., Attention: Permissions Department,
557 Broadway, New York, NY 10012.

ISBN 978-0-545-23101-5

Copyright © 2011 by Clare Hutton
All rights reserved. Published by Scholastic Inc.
SCHOLASTIC, POISON APPLE, and associated
logos are trademarks and/or registered
trademarks of Scholastic Inc.

12 11 10 9 8 7 6 5 4 3 2 1   11 12 13 14 15 16/0

Printed in the U.S.A.
First printing, February 2011

CHAPTER ONE

"You are going to *die*," my best friend Tasha said. Her brown eyes were wide with horror.

I laughed. "You're being ridiculous."

Tasha made a face. "You'll be lost out there. And I won't survive here without you."

We were sitting under a big oak tree on the grounds of our school, eating sandwiches from the café down the street. The sky was blue, the sun was warm, and a gentle breeze lifted strands of curly brown hair from my ponytail. It was a perfect September day.

School had been back in session for two weeks, and it seemed like Tasha and I had spent most of that time having the same conversation. Tomorrow,

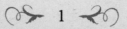

I was leaving our hometown of Austin, Texas, for three months.

"You love Austin!" Tasha insisted, tucking her chin-length black hair behind her ear and making a sad face at me. "And seventh grade has already started! We need to be study partners! And plan the Halloween Dance together!" She crumpled up her empty chip bag and looked at me, lips trembling. "Marisol, you *can't* leave. You won't be happy in the middle of nowhere."

Tasha is very, *very* dramatic. One day last year, she called me crying so hard she couldn't talk. I thought she was sick, or that something had happened to her family. I rushed over to her house on my bike, but it turned out she had just gotten a bad haircut. And it wasn't even that awful!

Tasha being her dramatic self made me reluctant to show any nerves at all: If I was the levelheaded one, I wasn't going to admit to any doubts about leaving town. And it's true I love Austin. It's the best city in the world — you can walk or bike pretty much everywhere; it's beautiful; and there are terrific restaurants, funky coffeehouses, great hiking trails, and cool music. But I wasn't leaving forever — I'd be back in just three months. I ignored the little tremor of nervousness in my stomach at the thought of leaving home, and took a big bite out of my sandwich.

I thought about how this totally unexpected trip had come about.

When my mom and I found out that everyone in our apartment building had to move out for a couple of months (the building needed a complete rewiring or it might catch fire — yikes!), I assumed we'd just rent another apartment in Austin.

Instead, my mom sat me down and told me she wanted to talk. I knew something big was coming.

"Marisol, I think we should go to Montana and live with Molly while they're fixing the wiring," she had said in a rush. Molly had been my mother's college roommate a long time ago. I'd never met her, but she and my mom got together for a girls' weekend in New York every couple of years, and she always sent us Christmas cards, so I'd *heard* of her. But still, it wasn't the most obvious solution to our problem.

When my mom explained her idea a little, it made more sense: Molly and her family run a bed-and-breakfast with horses (Yay! I could learn to ride!) in a little town called Wolf Valley near Glacier National

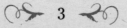

Park. Their busy season is summer, so they have plenty of room during the fall and winter. And Molly had been begging my mom to come out for a long visit for ages. Since my mom edits an online magazine, she can work anywhere, so that part made sense, too.

"This is such an amazing opportunity to experience life somewhere else!" my mom had said excitedly. "When are we going to have a chance to do this again? Pretty soon you're going to be in high school and won't be able to switch schools so easily, and then you'll go off to college. Now is the time!" Then she added casually, "And if we love it, we could even stay the rest of the school year! We'd have to help with the guests in the spring, but they don't get really busy until summer."

I had rolled my eyes. "Mom, this might be a great adventure, but I think I'll be ready to come home after three months of living with strangers."

My parents got divorced when I was eight, and my dad lives in Miami, so it didn't make any difference to him where my mom and I were. I spend part of my Christmas and summer vacations with him, so while it would be a longer plane ride to

Miami from Montana than from Austin, it was still a plane ride.

I'm a little less spontaneous than my mom, but spending a few months in Montana *did* sound like it could be awesome. I'd always lived in Austin, aside from visits to Miami and an occasional vacation. In Montana, I could try out a totally different life! How cool was that? So I had swallowed back my nerves and told myself my mom was right. This would be a great opportunity.

But, sitting on the lawn and looking at my best friend's sad face, I knew she wasn't going to be able to even pretend to get excited for me. I also knew that admitting even the smallest case of nerves would totally set Tasha off on another rant, which would only make me more anxious. I swallowed the last bite of my sandwich and reached out to squeeze her arm reassuringly. "Tasha, it's only for a few months. I'll be back before Christmas."

Tasha moaned and flopped down on her back, closing her eyes. "I'm afraid it's the end, Marisol. After three months in the middle of Nowhere, Montana, you'll be dead from boredom. What are you going to *do* out there?"

I flopped down next to her. The warm grass still smelled like summer. "I'm going to be fine. Montana will be great. I can hike and bike and explore out-doors. There'll be all kinds of animals, and can you imagine the night sky? We'll be out in the country, and the stars will be amazing without city lights. I'll be able to see things I've never seen before!" Austin's an outdoorsy city — there's a great park within walking distance of my building — but it's not the country. And I happen to love astronomy, so I was super-excited to use the telescope my dad had given me the previous Christmas out in the country.

Tasha made a face. She's into theater and dance and just barely tolerates the outdoors. Hiking and stargazing clearly didn't sound all that great to her. "Maybe the school won't let you go?" she asked hopefully.

"Nope, they're totally on board," I said. We go to the alternative public middle school in Austin. They're very committed to letting everyone pursue his or her own dreams (while meeting state require-ments, of course). "They're treating it like a semester abroad."

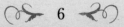

Tasha sighed and looked at me sadly. "I'm going to miss you."

Of course, I knew that was what she'd really been saying all along. Still, it was nice to hear it. I hugged her. "I'll miss you, too, Tash," I said. "But we'll both be fine. We'll talk and text and e-mail. Just think of it as if I'm on a long vacation."

I went to sleep that night with my bags packed, gazing up at the glow-in-the-dark stars on my ceiling and trying to think of it just that way: like a vacation. But as I lay in bed listening to the footsteps and laughter of passersby outside my building, I felt a cold shiver of anxiety. Now that I was alone, I had to admit that I *was* a little nervous. I mean, who wouldn't be? Sure, stepping into the unknown might be an awesome adventure, but it was also *scary*. I drifted off to sleep uneasily, a tense knot in my stomach.

A minute later, I was outdoors. The air was crisp and clear. I was walking along a wooded mountain path, brushing easily past the branches of wind-twisted trees. Dry leaves crunched under my feet. Above me, the sky darkened, but I wasn't worried about getting lost. I knew, in the way you always know things in dreams, that I was in Montana, exploring, and my heart was beating fast with excitement, not fear.

I reached a clearing in the woods and gazed upward. Cygnus, Aquila, and Ursa Major — familiar constellations — shone overhead, seeming so near I almost believed I could reach up and touch them. Just above the tops of the trees a huge, yellow full moon drifted in the sky.

Behind me, leaves rustled. I turned in time to see something disappearing into the undergrowth. Was it a cat?

I took a few steps forward. Yellow eyes gleamed at me from the bushes. A coyote? I crouched to peek beneath the bush. Whatever was in there whined — a thin, lost sound.

The breeze was rising, turning into a wind. On the wind, I heard Tasha's voice again. It was faint but clear, and much more ominous than her joking tone earlier: "You're going to die."

Suddenly, I was very afraid.

I started to run and, as I ran, I could hear something behind me, but I didn't want to look back.

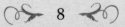

The path ended abruptly at the edge of a cliff. I wobbled at the brink, catching a dizzying glimpse of rocks and water far below before turning and looking back. I had to see what had been chasing me.

There was nothing there. And then I fell.

I woke up sweaty, my heart pounding. The clock said it was 2:17 in the morning. I thought of texting Tasha — she would be asleep, but just typing out a message might calm me down — or waking up my mom. Instead, I climbed out of bed and padded over to the window.

It was quiet outside. No one was walking by the building now. The streets were mostly empty, but occasionally a car drove past, its tires swooshing on the asphalt. The streetlights were on, and the calm city they illuminated helped me relax. Slowly, my breathing returned to normal.

"Montana's going to be great," I said to myself, but I didn't feel so sure.

CHAPTER TWO

The first thing I noticed about Montana was how *cold* it was. My mom and I stepped out of the tiny Glacier National Park International Airport, and suddenly the cute purple tank top and jeans, which had been perfect for a mid-September day in Austin, were *definitely* not enough.

I was exhausted. Turns out Glacier National Park Airport is impossible to fly to directly from Texas, so we'd spent a long, *long* time getting there.

Outside, the sky was a bright, clear blue, and I could see huge white-capped mountains not far in the distance.

"Wow!" I said, admiring the view. "Mom, check it out."

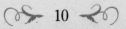

But my mom wasn't looking at the scenery. She had a big smile on her face and was waving wildly to a blond woman with long, frizzy hair and freckles. The woman was getting out of a red pickup truck near us and waving back with even more enthusiasm.

"Molly!" my mom practically screamed. "Molly!"

"Mom," I whispered, embarrassed. "She's about three feet away. You do not have to *yell*."

"ANA!" the woman — now only a foot away — shrieked back. She and my mom grabbed each other in a great big bear hug.

When they let go, Molly grabbed me and squeezed tight. She smelled like soap and just a little like horse. "Marisol!" she exclaimed. "I can't believe this is the first time I'm meeting you. You're so grown up!" She let go and turned to my mom. "Ana, she looks just like you did when we met."

They were off on a big round of remember-that-time when I noticed a girl about my age getting out of the truck. Her mom had leaped out and run over to us, looking delighted, but this girl was taking her time and wasn't smiling. She had long, frizzy blond hair, too, and freckles, and her pale blue eyes looked at me warily.

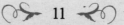

"Hi!" I said, stepping toward her. "I'm Marisol. Are you Molly's daughter?"

"Hailey," she mumbled, and hunched her shoulders, staring down at her shoes.

O . . . *kay*. Did she hate me already, or was she just shy?

I tried again. I gave her a big smile. "I can't believe my mom didn't tell me you were my age," I said. "All she said was 'Molly and her family.' You'd think she might have said, 'By the way, her daughter's the same age as you,' right?"

Hailey gave me a very small smile and then looked away.

My mom flushed. "I'm sorry, Molly, I hate to admit it, but I lost track of how old your twins are — I thought they were younger than Marisol, but they must be about the same age."

Molly nodded. "Hailey and Jack are twelve." She didn't seem offended that my mom hadn't known.

Wait a second. Twins? *Jack?*

My mother had also forgotten to tell me I was going to spend the next three months living with a *boy*.

To a lot of girls this would not be a big deal at all.

A lot of girls have brothers. Or guy friends they know really, really well and hang out with all the time, so they're like family.

But me? I'm a girl who lives with her mom and has close *girl* friends. I don't have any boy cousins, and I don't have any real guy friends. The last genuine friendship I had with a boy ended when Toby Collington stole my sparkly pencil in second grade and wouldn't give it back. I *knew* boys, of course, from school and stuff, but not super close-up. And definitely not *living together* close.

I try to be levelheaded in general. But that doesn't mean I'm fearless about extreme social weirdness, like sharing a bathroom with a boy. I started to panic. My first thought was: I'd need to stop wearing my pj's to breakfast. And I'd have to start brushing my hair before leaving my room in the morning.

I must have had a funny expression on my face, because Molly gave me a worried frown. "Marisol? Are you okay? Are you hungry?"

I smiled at her, relieved at an excuse to stop thinking about boys. "Actually, I'm starving!"

"Well, we'd better get going, then," she said cheerily, and led the way.

I made an awkward entrance into the backseat of the big pickup cab; it was hard to step up high enough, and I sort of scrambled my way onto the seat.

"Whoops," I said, laughing. "I don't have enough practice getting into pickups. We've got a hybrid back in Texas."

Hailey shrugged and looked away, out the window. *Hmmm,* I thought. *Really not friendly.*

Molly turned around from the front seat. "We've got about an hour and a half drive to our place. If you're starving, we should hit a drive-through before we leave town."

I looked out my window. There was a gorgeous view and not much else — just a few houses and a little strip mall with some stores and a McDonald's. "Where's town?" I asked.

Hailey stared at me but didn't say anything.

Molly laughed. "This is it!" she said, throwing her arms wide. "It doesn't look like much, but this is where we come to do our shopping. Out where we live is the real country."

"Wow," I said nervously. "That's . . . great. But I can't eat at McDonald's, I'm a vegetarian."

"What a coincidence!" said Molly cheerfully. "So is Hailey! You can just eat whatever she eats, and you'll be fine."

Hailey spoke for the first time since we'd gotten in the truck. "It *is* pretty tough to find something to eat in town," she said quietly. "I'm a vegan, so I don't even eat cheese. Most places, all I can get is a salad or maybe some fries."

"What about Chinese food?" I asked. "Or Indian? Veggie sushi? Tex-Mex?"

Hailey shook her head.

"Okay," I said weakly. If all I had for three months was salad and fries, then Tasha was right, I was definitely going to die — of malnutrition.

I shifted closer to Hailey and whispered. "We might have to starve here, but someday you'll come to Austin, and we'll get *real* food. Austin has the best Mexican food on the planet — well, the best outside of Mexico."

She gave me a startled look and flushed, turning to look out her window again. I sighed and leaned my head against my own window. Apparently, not eating meat hadn't been enough to break the ice.

Sure, I'd be fine — fine with a girl I had to live with and go to school with who would barely speak to me, fine living with a strange boy, fine with a diet consisting entirely of fried potatoes and iceberg lettuce. We had hardly left the airport, and I felt like my stay in Montana was doomed.

Chapter Three

I had to admit, the bed-and-breakfast was adorable. It was a giant log cabin, with little log cabins scattered around it in the woods. *Like the little cabins are the main house's babies,* I thought, grinning.

"Guest cabins," Molly said to my mom, waving one hand at them. "I'd put you and Marisol in one of those, Ana, but they get chilly in the off-season. And there's plenty of room in the house."

Beside the big log cabin, a cleared space surrounded a stable and riding ring. I could smell the faint scent of horses on the breeze. An immense green forest stood between the ranch and a mountain rising high against the horizon. The sky was wide and blue and cloudless.

I took a deep breath of fresh country air (and horses) and decided I was going to have a good time, no matter what. I put a smile on my face and headed for the house behind Molly and my mom. While I had been looking around, Hailey had taken off ahead of them.

A few steps from the front door, I stopped. Molly and my mom had gone inside, and I was alone. It was awfully quiet. In the distance, I heard a horse whinny.

I turned in a slow circle. Leaves rustled in the breeze, and everything was peaceful. But I had a strange feeling, like I was being watched. I held very still. *I'm imagining this,* I thought. *I'm tired, and the dream last night is making me nervous.*

A twig cracked in the tangled underbrush beside the road.

I hurried into the house, my heart racing.

The door opened into a cozy, warm kitchen, full of the smell of cooking food. As soon as I was inside, I had to laugh at myself. The boy chopping vegetables at the counter met my smile with a grin.

"Hey, how's it going?" he said. "I'm Jack."

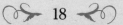

Jack was pretty cute. His very short blond hair, pale blue eyes, and freckles made it clear he was Hailey's brother, but his friendly smile made those features look totally different than they looked on Hailey's wary face.

"Hi," I said, feeling a little shy. "I like your house." It was really Western looking: log walls, paintings of horses, big cushy couches and chairs. It looked like a good place to curl up in front of a crackling fire after a long day riding the trails.

His dad came over and shook my mom's hand and smiled at me. "I'm Mike," he said. "We're real happy to have you visit. Molly's been so excited." He was a big, sweet-faced man. This family was all so friendly, except for Hailey. I couldn't figure her out.

"Can I help?" I asked Jack, who seemed to be cooking all by himself.

"Sure," he said. "Would you rather mix up the corn bread, rub the marinade into the steaks, or finish the salad?"

"Um," I hesitated. The idea of rubbing stuff into raw meat grossed me out. "I'll mix up the corn bread."

"Great!" He handed me a bowl. "Break an egg into this, and beat in a cup of milk and a quarter

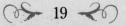

cup of vegetable oil. Then we'll mix it with the flour and stuff."

"Wow," I said, putting the bowl on the counter and getting out an egg. "You can really cook." I had the idea that boys thought cooking was unmanly. But, like I said, I don't actually know any boys.

"Yep," Jack said. "I want to be a chef." He was rubbing some oily stuff with dried leaves floating in it on the raw meat, and I had to look away. *Yuck!* I concentrated on beating the liquids together. "I'm in the cooking club at school — you should join! We practice recipes and go to restaurants, and we have a big party at the end of the semester."

"I don't know," I said awkwardly. "I'm better at eating than cooking."

"Marisol's a vegetarian like your sister," Molly told him. "Be sure to make extra salad."

"No problem," Jack said. "I'm making vegetable shish kebabs on the grill for Hailey, and we can make more for you. And there'll be plenty of corn bread, salad, and baked beans."

"That sounds great!" I said happily. I wasn't going to starve for three months after all. "Thank you!"

Jack handed off the skewers of vegetables and the steaks to his dad to put on the grill and finished

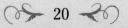

mixing up the corn bread and stuck it in the oven. Salad was in the bowl and baked beans were heating on the stove top. Molly and my mom were talking at the kitchen table.

I was sitting at a tall stool at the kitchen counter, and Jack pulled up a stool next to me.

"Um," he said, jiggling his knee. "So, if not cooking, what kind of stuff are you into? There's, like" — he waved his hand vaguely — "a lot of different things at school. Sports and art club and stuff. The girls' soccer team is pretty good."

"Maybe not soccer," I said. "I mean, I'm not that into team sports. I like lots of stuff, though. Hiking and biking, and animals, and being outdoors. And I'm interested in science, especially astronomy."

I felt like a dork saying that, but Jack perked right up. "Astronomy!" he said. "Awesome! There's an astronomy club at school. They have camping trips to look at the stars. Their fall trip is actually a big deal even for people who aren't in the club. Like, practically everybody goes."

"Really?!" I exclaimed. There was a science club at my school back home, and sometimes we talked about astronomy. We'd gone on a trip to the

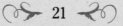

planetarium, but not enough kids were so interested in space that they'd want to join a club just for that.

"Sure," Jack said. "There's great stargazing around here. You can go out into Glacier National Park and take a telescope, or see a lot even just outside the house."

"This is going to be amazing," I told him.

"How'd you get into astronomy?" he asked curiously. "Like, is it a science thing, or an outdoorsy thing, or both?"

"Um, both, I guess," I said. "My dad bought a telescope for us to share when I was six, and we used to go out with it a lot. He'd show me all the different constellations."

"Neat," Jack said.

"Yeah," I said, smiling as I remembered stargazing with my dad. "Every year there's a big meteor shower in the summer called the Perseid shower, and he'd wake me up in the middle of the night to see it. We'd take a thermos of hot chocolate and go sit on the roof to watch the shooting stars. We still do it now that he lives in Miami; we try to make sure I'm out there at the right time."

"Sounds really nice," Jack said.

"Yeah, it is," I said again. I missed my dad now

that he lived in Miami. It was great to spend time with him on school breaks, but it wasn't the same as seeing him every day.

Our conversation hit a little pause, and Jack started looking around and jiggling his leg again. "Can you ride a horse?" he asked suddenly.

I shook off the thoughts about my dad. "Not really," I said apologetically. "The closest I got was a couple of rides on my friend's pony when I was eight. But I've always wanted to learn."

"You'd have a great time," he said. "I love it. I take people riding the trails around here all the time when we have guests, so if you want, we could go riding sometime. If you like animals and hiking, you'll be a natural. Our horses are really gentle."

"I don't think it's a great idea for Marisol to go out on a horse without an adult when she doesn't know how to ride," my mom broke in. I hadn't even realized she and Molly were listening to our conversation. "Maybe we could all go together sometime."

"Oh, Jack's a great teacher," Molly said dismissively. "She'll be fine."

My mom's lips tightened, but she didn't say anything. She gave me a look that meant *We'll discuss this later,* but I pretended not to see it. If Jack really took tourists out on horseback all the time, I didn't think my mother had anything to worry about.

The buzzer rang to let us know the corn bread was done just as Mike came in from outside carrying a platter. "Steaks and veggies are ready," he said. "Marisol, would you ask Hailey to come to the table?"

I glanced around. My mom was setting the table while Molly poured milk and water into big glasses. "Hailey's so moody these days," Molly said to my mom. "She's very self-conscious. Getting to be a teenager, right? I try to give her some space." My mom *mmmm*ed in agreement.

Jack was getting the corn bread out of the oven, but he rolled his eyes at me. "I like how parents blame everything they don't like on our age," he said pointedly. "Hailey's room is upstairs. Just look for the wolf doorknocker."

"Thanks," I said, and headed upstairs.

The hall was dark, and a line of light shone around the edges of Hailey's door. I hesitated, then knocked.

There was no sound from behind the door. Was

she there? Should I knock again? I would feel stupid standing in the dark outside her door if she had headphones on or was in the bathroom or something. I waited and waited and then finally raised my hand to knock again.

Suddenly, the door flew open.

"What?" Hailey asked.

I looked past her and my mouth dropped open. I couldn't tell what color her walls were because everywhere, from floor to ceiling, there were images of animals: pictures printed off websites, cut out of magazines, and on posters. Lion cubs wrestled playfully. A raccoon clung to a tree branch. Horses galloped over dunes. A hundred different animals were playing, hunting, eating, and basking in the sun. The largest poster of all showed a line of wolves coming over the crest of a hill, their cool amber gazes watchful and calm. Looking in from the dark hall, it was as if Hailey's door had opened into the wild.

"What?" Hailey asked again. "Please, my room is *private*." She stepped out into the hall and closed the door behind her.

I realized I had been staring, which was pretty rude. "Oh, sorry . . . wow, it's like a zoo in there!"

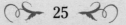

Hailey ducked her head. "I really like animals," she said softly. "I don't like zoos, though. Wild animals should be free."

"Um, I can understand how you feel," I said. I paused, but neither of us seemed to have anything more to say. "Anyway, dinner's ready."

She followed me down the hall toward the kitchen so quietly I almost turned around to make sure she was still behind me. I just wanted her to *say* something. Hailey seemed kind of intense, and she made me a little uncomfortable.

I was starving when I sat down at the table. Jack set a plate in front of me with a flourish.

"Hey, this looks really good," I said, digging in. The veggies from the shish kebab were tasty: juicy and warm and flavored with different herbs.

"This steak is perfect, Mike and Jack!" my mom exclaimed from the other end of the table. "Absolutely delicious."

"The corn bread didn't turn out so well," Jack said, gazing at a bread basket full of blackened slices. "It got kind of scorched."

He looked sad. I reached out and grabbed a piece of corn bread. "I'm sure it'll be fine with a little butter," I said cheerfully. I slathered on some butter and

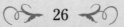

took a big bite. It was surprisingly edible. "The unburned parts are delicious," I said, chewing. Jack laughed.

Later that night, Hailey led me up to show me my room, which was down the hall from hers.

I smiled at her. "Dinner was great. Jack's a good cook."

She shrugged. "Sure."

"I guess I won't starve out here after all," I joked. "Maybe I can even get Jack to learn how to make vegetarian sushi." Hailey made a strange noise and turned away from me into her own room.

I stared after her. Had she just *growled* at me?

CHAPTER FOUR

The next morning, I woke up early and lay in bed, trying to remain calm. I took a deep breath and let it out slowly, staring at the ceiling. It was my first day at Wolf Valley Middle School, and I was scared to death. What if everyone hated me?

It's only for three months, I told myself.

Three months sounded a *lot* longer now than it had when I agreed to this trip.

At least I have Jack, I thought finally, and that helped me sit up. Having one friend already was going to be a lifesaver. If it weren't for him, I might have tried to convince my mom to let me stay in bed all day.

It was funny how in just one evening I'd gone from being totally freaked out by the idea of living with a boy to being happy that he was my friend. Jack was nice: relaxed and funny and easy to be around. Cute, too. But I shook that thought off — crushing on a boy I was living with would be way too complicated.

I pulled myself together. I was Marisol Perez! I was *fearless*!

Sort of fearless.

I hopped out of bed and headed for the shower. My personal shower, which was a huge perk after sharing a bathroom with my mom my whole life. Turns out one of the biggest benefits of staying at an off-season bed-and-breakfast is that there are plenty of bedrooms to choose from, all with their own bathrooms. My room looked like a fancy hotel room: flowery bedspread and wallpaper, matching lamps on either side of the double bed, and a little desk with brochures and books about the area: *The Birds of Western Montana*, *Hiking the Glaciers*, and *The Wolves of Wolf Valley*. The decor was definitely *not* what I would have chosen, but it was comfortable and all mine.

Half an hour later, I was clean, my hair looked good, I was wearing lip gloss (the only makeup my mom will let me use), and I had on jeans and a blue sweater. I was as ready as I'd ever be. I tried to text Tasha so she could wish me good luck, but my cell phone didn't have a signal.

When I got to the kitchen, Jack and Hailey were sitting at the table, eating cereal, while my mom and Molly drank coffee. I slid into my seat on the other side of the table and gave them a shaky smile.

"It's weird that I'm starting school almost a month late, right?" I asked nervously.

"Don't worry about it," Jack said through a mouthful of cereal. He swallowed and spoke more clearly. "By now, everybody's sick of seeing all the same people every day. They'll be thrilled to have someone new around. You'll be a total celebrity."

Hailey's hair was tied back in a braid, making her look more approachable than she had the day before. To my complete shock, she smiled at me and said in a soft voice, "It'll be fine, really."

Maybe she's just shy, I thought, and smiled back at her. "Yeah," I agreed. "And after all, what do I care what people here think of me anyway?" Like I had been telling myself, I wasn't going to be here long enough for it to really matter.

Hailey's smile snapped shut and she got up from the table. "We need to catch the bus," she said flatly. She didn't look at me as she kissed her mother good-bye.

"What'd I say?" I whispered to Jack as we followed her out the door.

"Don't worry about it," he whispered back. "Hailey's moody. She likes animals more than she likes people." While we waited for the bus at the end of the drive, Jack stood with his sister, murmuring to her in a low voice. She glanced over at me, and I stepped back and looked away, trying to give them some privacy, since they were obviously talking about me.

By the time the big yellow school bus pulled up, I was so uncomfortable that I was actually relieved to see it.

That is, until I got up the bus stairs and saw a bunch of strange faces staring at me. *Fearless*, I thought, and tried to look nonchalant as I hurried into the empty seat behind the driver. I thought Jack might sit next to me, but he went past me to sit with some guys at the back of the bus. Hailey gave me a brief, reluctant smile but walked past me, too, to sit alone a couple of seats farther back.

I didn't know what my friendship possibilities were going to be like at school, but apparently I wasn't all that popular with the people I was living with.

My school in Austin is modern: one story, full of windows and bright colors. Here, the school was tall, brick, and old-fashioned looking, with steps up to the front and two front doors, one that said GIRLS over it and another saying BOYS. I grabbed Hailey's arm as she tried to walk past me.

She jumped like I'd really startled her. "What?" she asked.

"Just tell me," I said. "Do I have to go in the one that says GIRLS? Or doesn't it matter?"

"It doesn't matter," Hailey said. She looked at her feet and added in a soft voice, "Come on, I'll show you to the office."

After I picked up my schedule, the rest of the morning was a blur. The school was bigger than I'd expected; kids were bused in from all over the county. I kept getting turned around in the halls. Jack was in my homeroom and English classes, and introduced me to a bunch of people whose names I forgot right away. Hailey was in my math class and

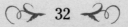

gave me a brief wave from across the room, then sat and drew in her notebook for the entire period.

During study hall, I sat alone at a round table in the library. All around me, kids were whispering, sharing books, and laughing quietly. I felt gigantically out of place. I watched a girl with a long, honey-colored braid fold a note into an origami flower and hand it to her friend, and I wanted to cry.

"Ten minutes only on the computers, people," the teacher said, clapping her hands to get attention. "Give someone else a turn."

I jumped up fast, almost knocking my backpack off the table, and grabbed one of the newly vacated computers.

Logging on to my e-mail, I saw I had a bunch of messages from my friends back home. There were e-mails from Tasha, Ashley, and Erica, whom I ate lunch with, and from Kayla in my math class. They all said mostly the same things: *miss u, luv u, hope you're having fun.* And there were bits of gossip: who had a crush on whom, who had gotten into trouble with her parents, and who said what to a teacher.

Reading them made me feel stronger. So what if I

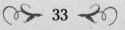

didn't have friends here? I had friends back in my real life.

And if people liked me back in Austin, probably somebody would like me in Wolf Valley, too.

I e-mailed Tasha back quickly, because my ten minutes were almost up:

To: diva12@netmail.com
From: stargirl1013@netmail.com

Hi, Tasha,
Montana is beautiful. Guess what my mom forgot
to tell me: her friend has two kids our age!
They're nice, especially Jack (a GUY! Yikes!). My
phone doesn't work here.
I miss you! Talk soon!
xoxo

E-mailing Tasha cheered me up, but by lunchtime I was lonely again. It was *hard* being the new kid. Nobody had been mean to me — everyone was pretty friendly — but they all knew one another and were wrapped up in their own friendships. After politely saying hello, people pretty much ignored me. I missed Tasha and my other friends. And I

missed just already knowing people instead of having to meet everyone for the first time.

Lunch is scary when you have no friends, because there are no assigned seats in the cafeteria. And if no one talks to you, you can't just listen to the teacher, because there is no teacher.

Back home, we could eat outside on the school grounds, but at Wolf Valley everyone ate in the cafeteria. I pulled my shoulders back and stood up straight before walking in, repeating *fearless* to myself, but not really believing it.

At first, the cafeteria seemed like one big buzz of strangers' conversations and tons of seats, all filled. I almost turned around and walked right back out.

Then I saw a girl smiling at me, waving and pointing at an empty seat at her table. She looked familiar — she was one of the people Jack had introduced me to (thank you, Jack!) — but I had no idea what her name was. She was athletic-looking, with dark brown hair pulled back into a ponytail and a big smile.

"Hey!" she said. "Marisol, right? Come sit with us."

"Thanks," I said. I sat down, and there was a little silence as I looked at her and her friends and they looked at me. One of her friends had short, curly red hair and big blue eyes. The other one was the girl from the library who had twisted a note into a flower. She had long hair. "I'm really sorry," I said. "I've met two of you before, but I can't remember either of your names. This whole day has been a total blur." They all smiled.

"I'm Amber," said the athletic-looking girl, "and this is Bonnie." The redheaded girl smiled and gave me a little wave. "And this is Lily," Amber said. The long-haired girl nodded.

"I'm sure it's been a really long morning," Bonnie said as she bounced in her seat enthusiastically. "Is starting so late and not knowing anybody *killing* you? We felt sorry for you and thought you looked like you needed somewhere to sit."

"Bonnie!" said Amber, but she was laughing, too. "Don't tell her that."

"I didn't mean to hurt your feelings," Bonnie said anxiously. "I didn't, did I?"

"Of course not," I said. I got out my brown paper bag and started unpacking my lunch. Peanut butter sandwich, tangerine, and cookies. The other girls all had cafeteria trays with burgers on them.

Bonnie giggled. "Only weird people, or people

with serious food issues, pack their lunch here. The cafeteria food isn't *that* bad."

"Bonnie!" Amber said again. I could tell she was the bossy one. Lily just sat and watched us eat.

"Sorry again," Bonnie said. "I wasn't saying you're a weirdo, I was just saying you should know what people do here."

"Um." I looked at my sandwich. Did people really think you were weird if you didn't eat the cafeteria lunch? Did I care? "I'm a vegetarian, so I kind of have to bring my lunch."

"Oh!" Bonnie said. "My dad would kill me if I stopped eating meat. We raise cattle."

Amber smiled at me. "I like veggies. Lily's a total carnivore, though."

Lily nodded seriously. "I like meat a lot."

"That's fine with me," I said. "I mean, I don't mind other people eating it, it's just sort of not my thing."

They let the subject drop, and we talked about other stuff: Austin, and what kids did for fun in Wolf Valley, and TV shows, and people I didn't know yet but would know a lot of gossip about when I finally met them.

"And of course, you're totally lucky to live with Jack McManus," Bonnie said. "He is such a cutie. I actually joined the cooking club to admire him, which is a joke because I can hardly boil water."

"Mmm," I said noncommittally. "Jack's nice. Are you all in the cooking club?"

"Just Bonnie," said Amber. "I don't have time for other clubs, with student government — which is a very serious deal here — and the field hockey and volleyball teams. And Lily's into science. She's in the astronomy and ecology clubs."

"Really?" I practically shouted. Lily blinked at me. "I'm dying to join the astronomy club! I was so excited to hear there is one."

"Oh," Lily said. She thought it over and gave me a slow smile. "There's a meeting right after school today. We meet every Monday. You should come."

By the time the bell rang, I was feeling much better than when I had walked into the cafeteria. I had three potential friends, I was going to join a club, and I had conquered the terrors of a new school's lunch period. Once again, I felt fearless.

CHAPTER FIVE

After school, I called my mom from the pay phone by the office; my cell didn't work at school either. Looking at the mountains surrounding the town, I figured I might as well give up trying to use my phone in Wolf Valley. When I asked my mom about staying for astronomy club, she hesitated.

"Marisol, I'm glad you found something you enjoy at school already, but I haven't rented a car yet. Molly and Mike are being really generous letting us stay here. I don't think we should ask them to make special trips to drive you around."

Luckily, I had talked to Jack in social studies that afternoon, and he'd told me that he was staying for cooking club. Not only would he also need a late ride home, there was actually an activities bus that

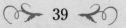

would drop us off. So I could tell my mom that no one was going to have to make a special trip for me. Once she stopped worrying that I was going to be a bad guest, she was really excited that Wolf Valley had an astronomy club.

"See?" she said. "I knew this was going to be a great semester!"

"Whatever, Mom," I said, laughing. "It's only been one day." But I was happy.

I felt shy again when I found Room 204, where the astronomy club meeting was being held. There were about fifteen kids milling around, and the only one I recognized was Lily. She was sitting at a desk, flipping through a notebook. There was a teacher at the back of the room, but he had his head down and looked like he was correcting papers, not getting ready to start the meeting.

"*New* girl," said a boy standing near the door. He looked me up and down. "Come on in." He bared his teeth at me, showing me his braces and a chunk of green stuff caught in them. "We're ready for some *new* blood." He put his arm over the lower half of his face and did a vampire impression. "Wah-ha-ha-ha."

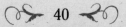

Lily looked up. "Shut up, Anderson," she said, and smiled at me. "Hi, Marisol. Come sit with me."

The boy with the braces mimicked her. "*Shut up, Anderson, shut up, Anderson.* When is Anderson going to feel the love?" But he stopped bothering me.

I sat down at the desk next to Lily's. "Thanks," I said, relieved.

"No problem," she replied with a smile. "We're just about ready to get started. I'm the president, so let me tell you about the meetings."

I glanced at the teacher at the back of the room. "Oh," said Lily. "Mr. Samuels just shows up because we need a club sponsor. He's not that interested in astronomy. We really run the club ourselves.

"So . . ." She slapped a piece of paper down on the desk in front of me. Looking down, I saw a list that read:

Fabric of Space
Steady State versus Expanding Universe
Human Space Exploration
Eclipses
Star Types/Star Life Cycle
Comets

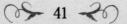

"These are some ideas for topics," Lily said. "Every week someone gives a presentation. If there's something else you want to talk about that's not on the list, that's okay, too. Um, unless it's not about astronomy. Somebody wanted to give a presentation on star signs and romance one time, which wasn't really the same thing."

She giggled a little as she put down another piece of paper, which had another neat list of topics, each with a person's name next to it. I saw that today someone named Becka Thompson was giving a presentation on black holes.

"Wow," I said. "You're really organized." I was surprised: Lily had been quiet at lunch and seemed like she took her time at everything, even smiling. I hadn't thought of her as a take-charge kind of person. The science club I was in back in Austin was totally run by the teacher, not the students.

As Lily straightened the papers, I noticed a small golden-brown birthmark on her arm in the shape of a crescent moon. It was unusual, and sort of pretty. The moon shape was so perfect for the president of the astronomy club that I almost said something like "Hey, with a moon birthmark you'll never have to get a tattoo." Luckily, I bit it back at the last minute. She might not think it was funny, and the last thing I needed was someone else here thinking I was weird (clearly Hailey already did).

"I'll do comets," I told her. "But give me a few weeks." I wasn't thrilled about the idea of talking in front of a bunch of strangers, but I would worry about that later.

She wrote me down for a date in November, then stood up and looked around. "Guys?" she said. Everyone stopped talking and turned to her. "Becka?" she called out. "You're up! Becka's talking about black holes, everybody."

A skinny girl with messy black curls went to the front of the room and shifted uncomfortably from foot to foot. "Um," she said. "Well, black holes are places with such strong gravity that nothing can escape, not even light."

She went on, and, as she talked, she relaxed and spoke more easily. She knew a lot about her topic, and had even brought illustrations from the Hubble Space Telescope website.

The amazing thing was how interested everyone was. No one was whispering, or napping, or passing notes. They were listening and raising their hands to ask questions. Back home, kids at a science club meeting would have been mostly interested, but someone probably would have been zoning out, and someone else would have been passing notes. It wasn't always easy to pay attention after a long day of school.

Because my dad and I studied it together, astronomy was really special to me, even back when I was a little kid. My friends in science club back home *liked* science, and a lot of them were *interested* in astronomy, but not like I was.

I felt a thrill of delight. Here in Montana, I had fallen into some kind of alternate universe, where everyone liked science just as much as I did.

When Becka finished talking, we applauded, and Lily got up. "That was awesome," she said. "Thanks, Becka. Next week, Tyler's talking about exoplanets. Yay!" She gathered up some of the papers on her desk. "Okay, moving on to announcements. As you know, our trip to Glacier National Park is two weeks from Friday. If friends want to join us, that's great. It's lots of fun, and the more people who go, the cheaper the trip is for everyone. There's a full moon tonight, so it should be waxing gibbous and almost full again then. If it's not raining, that'll be nice."

Now that we were talking about a field trip instead of black holes, Mr. Samuels got to his feet. "If you haven't gotten a permission slip, see me," he said sternly. "No one can attend the field trip without a signed form from their parents. And remember — only students who attend this school can join us on the field trip. No friends from outside." Everyone started getting their stuff together, and I hurried over to Mr. Samuels to get a permission slip. When I finished talking to him, I found Lily waiting for me.

"So, what'd you think?" she said.

"It was great," I answered enthusiastically. "I can tell I'm going to have to find out a lot about comets if I'm going to talk without totally embarrassing myself, though."

"Are you taking the activities bus?" Lily asked as she picked up her pink backpack.

"Yup," I said. "Are you?"

She nodded. "We'd better hurry to catch it."

I felt ridiculously pleased with myself: At the beginning of the day, I hadn't known anyone but Jack and Hailey, and now I was walking down the hall with a potential friend after a club meeting, just as if I'd been at this school forever.

"Tell me about the camping trip," I said.

"It's awesome," Lily replied, her eyes sparkling. "We take a ton of kids for a weekend in Glacier National Park. We bring telescopes and look at constellations, the moon, Jupiter, Venus — everything that's visible. Last year, we also read myths about the moon and stars. A bunch of teachers chaperone, and we roast marshmallows and do the whole campout thing. I'm pretty sure Jack and his friends are already signed up, and so are Amber and Bonnie. You should totally come."

"I definitely will," I said. "I mean, assuming my mom lets me, but I don't know why she wouldn't."

The skinny boy with the braces who'd been all "new girl, new girl" caught up and walked with us. "I can't *wait* for the trip," he said. "I've got a ghost story I've been working on. It's going to have the sixth graders running home to their mommies."

Lily sighed. "Anderson, do you mind? We're having a conversation here." I couldn't believe it, but he actually stopped talking. She turned to me. "Do you have a telescope? We try to bring as many as we can so everybody gets to use them."

"Yeah, I've got one. I'll be glad to bring it on the trip," I said. I had lugged it along as a carry-on on

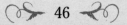

the plane, even though my mom thought I should leave it at home. "I didn't realize there was a full moon tonight until you said so. Maybe I'll set up the telescope outside. I haven't gotten a chance to use it here yet, and the stars are way more visible than at home."

Lily frowned. "Oh . . . it's not really the best idea to go out alone at night right around Wolf Valley. Especially during a full moon."

I stopped walking. "How come?"

Anderson started to laugh and lurched toward me with his hands crooked into claws. "Because of the *werewolves*," he said menacingly.

CHAPTER SIX

"Werewolves?" I looked uncertainly back and forth between Lily and Anderson. This was obviously some kind of joke, but I didn't get it.

Lily rolled her eyes. "There's no such thing as a werewolf, Anderson," she said flatly.

"That's what you say," Anderson said, grinning. "Everyone knows that Wolf Valley is stalked by werewolves. How do you think it got its name?"

Lily frowned. "Um, from wolves?"

"Yeah, unusually large and intelligent wolves," Anderson replied. He turned to me. "Hunters are allowed to kill wolves here, but only during wolf hunting season. And they can only kill, like, seventy-five in the whole state, and then the season closes."

"Yuck," I said. "I hate hunting."

"Anyway," he went on, "all year long, people see huge wolves in this area. Especially at night. And especially around the full moon. So hunters come here during wolf hunting season, and some people around here get wolf licenses, but *no one ever kills a single wolf.* They always just disappear. And then, once hunting season is over, they're back. Does that sound normal to you? Do normal *wolf* wolves know how to read a calendar?"

I looked at Lily skeptically. Was this guy kidding?

She shrugged. "Coincidence. Anderson's overstating how often people see wolves around here. People hear them, but they hardly ever see them. Students from the university camp out around here to see wolves in what should be peak wolf season, and I don't think they've ever seen one. And with only seventy-five wolves allowed to be killed anywhere in the state before they close the season, it would be statistically more surprising for a hunter to actually shoot one than not."

"Oh yeah?" Anderson said. "Where did all the werewolf stories about Wolf Valley come from, then? My grandfather told me his own grandmother saw a huge wolf get shot in the leg, a long time ago, and the next day, *her neighbor was limping.*"

Lily and I stared at him, then glanced at each other and burst out laughing.

"Anderson," she said between giggles, "that is the weakest story I've ever heard."

We were still laughing when we got on the bus. Lily and I sat together, and Anderson flopped into the seat behind us. Jack was in the back, sitting with some other guys, and he tipped me a little wave.

"Stop laughing at me," Anderson groused. "There are lots of other stories, too, from people who've actually seen werewolves. If we found somebody with the werewolf signs, we could watch them around the full moon."

"Like what?" I asked him. "What are werewolf signs?"

He straightened up, looking pleased that I was interested. "A long ring finger," he said. "Pointed ears. Heavy eyebrows."

Lily made a *pfft* noise and waved him away. "Please," she said, "Anyone could have any of those things. *I* have pointed ears." She pulled her hair back to show us, and her ears were kind of pointy on top.

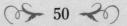

"And I'm not a werewolf, am I? And my ring fingers are pretty long, too."

I looked at her hands. The ring fingers didn't look superlong to me.

"Well . . ." Anderson frowned at her. "The eyebrows are the most commonly accepted sign."

"Maybe I pluck them. You'd never know, would you?" Lily smirked at him. Then she turned back to me, and her face got serious. "Marisol, even though there's no such thing as a werewolf, there *are* wolf packs in the area, and people around here stay indoors at night. So don't go wandering around unless you're with a big group of people, okay?"

I nodded. I shivered when I remembered how I had felt when I had been outside alone my first evening in town.

The bus dropped Jack and me off at the end of the long driveway up to the house, and I walked quickly and nervously. It was past four o'clock. Later in the year, it would be dark by this time, and now that I knew that the forest all around was crawling with wolves, I really wasn't looking forward to making this walk in the dark. I was glad I wasn't alone, but I doubted Jack would be much protection from a pack of wolves.

"What's up?" asked Jack. He jogged to catch up. "How was the meeting?"

"Great," I said, speeding up even more. "Let's get inside." I felt a tingling at the back of my neck, like someone was watching me, and I turned to peer into the shadows in the trees by the driveway. Were the eyes of something (a wolf? a werewolf?) glinting in there? I shivered, grabbed Jack's arm, and pulled him along the last few yards to the door.

Hailey was doing her homework at the kitchen table when we came in.

"What's *up*?" Jack asked, pulling his arm out of my hand, half-laughing, half-annoyed. "Are you okay?"

"Sorry, I'm just a little nervous," I said. "Have you heard that there are wolves around here?"

Jack grinned and cocked his head toward Hailey. "You should ask her about them. She's the wildlife expert." Hailey crossed her arms in front of her and stared at me. I thought about how the walls of her room were covered with animal pictures. She didn't look like she was planning on giving me any information, though.

"Hailey," I said, super-politely, "please tell me about the wolves."

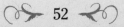

Hailey shrugged. "I don't know what you want to know," she said reluctantly. "There's definitely at least one wolf pack around here — people have spotted them and seen their tracks. They estimate there might be as many as fifteen wolves, which is a pretty large pack. But they must roam a big area, because nobody knows where their den is, and it can be months between sightings."

"Have they ever attacked anyone?" I asked, morbidly fascinated. "Lily told me not to go out alone with my telescope."

Hailey frowned. "Wolves don't attack people," she said sharply. "That is, unless they're cornered or starving."

Jack rummaged through the kitchen cupboard and pulled out a bag of chips. "They've killed animals, though," he said. "Sheep and cows. The ranchers hate them."

"Nobody knows for sure that was the wolf pack," Hailey objected. "It could have been stray dogs." Jack shrugged but didn't answer.

"And, um . . ." I felt like an idiot. "One of the kids said something about werewolves?"

Jack laughed. "Was it Anderson?" he asked, and laughed again when I nodded. "He's always got a wacky theory about something," he said. "There have been stories about werewolves around here for years, but no one takes them seriously."

"There's no such thing as werewolves," Hailey said. I started to agree, but she kept talking. "It's too bad, though. Wolves are amazing. They're graceful and courageous and loyal — they're a lot of things that humans ought to be. Maybe it would do the human race good if some people *were* werewolves."

Hailey was frowning defiantly, but her eyes were shining, and I had a sudden flash of warmth toward her. *Graceful, courageous, loyal* — someone who was so passionate about these qualities was worth trying to be friends with.

I took a deep breath and plunged in. "Hailey?" I said. "I feel like we got off to a bad start. I know I made you mad, but I don't know what I did. Can we try again? I'd like to be friends."

For a minute, Hailey was very still. "I don't know what you're talking about," she said. I stared at her, and she stared back, blue eyes wide.

Jack smacked the table, making us both jump. "Hailey!" he said sternly. "Marisol is trying. Give her a chance." I gave him a little smile, but he was busy glaring at his sister.

Hailey sighed, and when she looked at me, her eyes softened. "Listen, Marisol," she said. "You said some things that were kind of snotty, like you were looking down on us for living in the country." She fiddled with the edge of her notebook. "Anyway, I was nervous about having you come and stay here, and it hurt my feelings."

I was totally dumbfounded. "Like what? What did I say?" I could hear my voice getting louder and squeakier.

"Like that it didn't matter what people here thought of you. Or like when you acted surprised that you couldn't get *sushi* in town. Or when you were surprised we had a pickup instead of a *hybrid*."

"Oh," I said. Honestly, I thought Hailey was being way too sensitive. But I was glad to find out why she'd been acting so cold toward me, and that it was nothing horrible, just a misunderstanding.

"I'm sorry, Hailey," I said. "I didn't mean to sound that way. I really like it here. When I said it didn't matter what people thought of me, I only said that because I'm leaving soon. I meant that if no one likes me, it's okay because at least I don't have to stay. And I didn't mean it, anyway — I do want people to like me." I thought of Hailey sitting alone in the

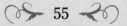

classroom and felt myself blush a little bit. I didn't think she had a lot of friends. "And anything else was just me being kind of a dork. Which I am, sometimes."

Hailey frowned down at her notebook and then looked up at me and smiled. "Okay," she said. "I'm sorry, too. I should have been nicer to you."

It was like a huge weight had lifted off my shoulders. I hadn't realized just how much living with somebody who disliked me had been bothering me.

Jack rolled his eyes at both of us. "Well, I'm glad that's over," he said simply. "Did you get the social studies assignment?"

My warm and fuzzy feelings toward Hailey continued for the rest of the evening. After dinner, we all hung out with our parents for a while, playing board games. Hailey turned out to be a star at Cranium.

As the evening got later, though, Hailey became jumpy and distracted. Her knee was vibrating, she was bouncing in her seat, and she kept missing her turn.

"What's going on with you?" Jack asked her when she forgot to roll the dice for the third time in a row.

"Hmmm?" Hailey asked, tapping her fingers on

the table and glancing quickly out the window. I turned to look: nothing but darkness.

"Sheesh," said Jack as he pushed back his chair and stood. "If no one's paying attention to the game, I'm going to get ready for bed."

"I will, too," Hailey said, jumping to her feet.

As they went upstairs, our mothers exchanged an amused look.

"I'm glad the girls are getting along better," my mom said cheerfully.

"Still right here," I reminded them. They just laughed.

I checked my e-mail on the family computer in the living room. Tasha had e-mailed me back:

To: stargirl1013@netmail.com
From: diva12@netmail.com

Two kids our age! A GUY?! You left out the important part: is he CUTE? Is she nice? You still like me best, right?

I replied:

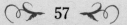

Jack's supercute, but I plan to like him like a brother. And Hailey's nice, but not as nice as you. I made a couple of other potential friends today, too. I think I may like Montana (but Austin forever!).

Then I said good night to my mom, Molly, and Mike, and headed for bed.

I was halfway down the hall, passing Hailey's room, when I heard it.

Aaaawwww-oooooo.

My heart pounded. Was that a wolf howl? It came again, and the little hairs on my neck stood on end.

Aaaaawwww-ooooooo.

Just as well I'm not out there with a telescope, I thought.

It was amazing, though. The call sounded so wild and lonely. Based on what she'd said earlier, I knew one person who would be blown away by it, and I wondered whether she had heard it, too.

I knocked on Hailey's door.

After a moment, I knocked again. It hadn't been

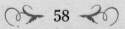

long enough since she went upstairs for her to be asleep.

I remembered waiting in the dark outside her room the night I had arrived, and how she'd said fiercely that her room was private, but we were friendly now, right? I turned the knob.

The lights were out and Hailey's window was wide open, a cold breeze rustling the pictures on the wall. The full moon shone in, illuminating enough that I could see the shapes of the furniture.

"Hailey?" I asked, taking a tentative step inside. Maybe she had gone to sleep already after all.

But Hailey's bed was empty. She hadn't been in the hall or on the stairs. I would have passed her if she had gone anywhere, except maybe my room. I ran down the hall quickly and checked. Hailey wasn't there.

I remembered Hailey staring out the window at the darkness, and I remembered the cold chill at the back of my neck that afternoon as I'd walked up the drive.

The wolf's howl rang out again, clear in the cold night air.

Aaaaah-wwwwooooo.

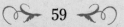

CHAPTER SEVEN

I didn't know what to do. Part of me wanted to go grab my mom and Hailey's parents, shriek that Hailey was missing and that there were wolves outside, and let them handle it. But I had just started being friends with Hailey, and if she was secretly raiding the kitchen and I had missed her on the stairs, I didn't want to get her in trouble. Besides, I would look like a panicky idiot.

She was probably just talking to Jack before she went to bed. I held on to that idea like it was a life preserver. It was reasonable, it was nonscary, and it was totally believable. *Yes, she's talking to her brother.*

Still, I left the door to my room open so that I would hear her when she came back. I sat in the flowery armchair in my room where I could get a view of the hall in case she passed by. We were reading *The Giver* for English class, and I tried to fill up my time by reading ahead, but I couldn't concentrate. After a few minutes, I hopped up and wandered restlessly around my room.

Among the brochures about the area on my desk was a thin book called *The Wolves of Wolf Valley*. I hadn't looked at it before. I had assumed it was a wildlife guide, but now that I looked at it more closely, it didn't look like a wildlife guide. Don't those usually have pictures?

"Weird," I muttered. I flipped it open and began to read:

In the earliest days of Wolf Valley,
settlers spent uneasy nights haunted by
the howls of wolf packs wandering the
streets of their newly established town.
Children and livestock were kept inside
for fear of the ravenous beasts. But the
worst was yet to come, as the horrified
settlers learned the legends told by the
nearby native tribes . . . the stories of
half men, half wolves who stalked

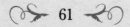

the mountains and woods near their new home.

The book went on to tell how eight hunters went out one night to hunt down the wolves endangering their town, and only three returned. Soon, the rest of the townspeople noticed weird changes in those three men and their families. From the time of the hunt, they seemed hostile and wary of their neighbors. They got hairier, their ears became more pointed, and they were said to eat their meat raw. *(Ew!)*

Eventually, rumors spread that these families were changing into wolves when the moon was full. There were stories like the one Anderson's grandfather told him, about a wolf being shot and a human showing up wounded the next day. Some people even claimed they had witnessed humans changing into wolves, in the woods or outside houses in the dark.

Legend said that the hunters had been cursed by the mystical wolves of the valley. They had ventured into the wild, and the wild had changed them. The town lived in fear.

One night, someone burned down the houses of

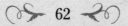

the families suspected of being werewolves. The book said that no one knew for sure who had done it, but it seemed like the whole town must have been behind it. The three families disappeared and were rumored to have moved farther into the wilderness. The book went on:

> The three families were never seen again, but Wolf Valley is still the haunt of a large number of wolves, wolves whose numbers increase at the time of the full moon. But now we know that there are no such beasts as werewolves. Nothing supernatural lurks in the woods around Wolf Valley . . . or does it?

"Weird," I muttered again, and shivered. I glanced outside, where the full moon hung in the sky. It suddenly seemed menacing. I got up and pulled down the shade.

It was getting late when I finally climbed into bed, sure I wouldn't be able to sleep. I lay awake for a long time listening, but I didn't hear a sound from Hailey's room. The wolf seemed to have moved on, because I didn't hear it howl again. It felt like I waited

for hours, but when I finally fell asleep, Hailey still hadn't come back.

I was walking the same path through the forest as in my previous dream. It was colder than before, and the wind whipped the tree branches back and forth, making clawing black shadows in the pale moonlight.

The full moon hung just over the horizon, swollen and yellow like an overripe fruit. Leaves crunched beneath my feet.

It was the same path, but this time I was not the happy explorer. I didn't want to walk forward, but I couldn't stop myself or turn back. My mouth was dry with fear. Something was going to happen. Something new. Something horrible. There was a crackle of dry branches in the undergrowth. Suddenly, a dirty, scratched figure stumbled onto the path in front of me, falling forward onto her hands and knees, long blond hair hiding her face. As she struggled to get to her feet, I saw that it was Hailey. She was panting hard, and after half-rising, she fell back to her knees. I tried to reach out to her, but I couldn't move.

She twisted in pain. Then her face lengthened, her nose and chin growing together into a kind of

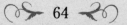

snout. Her body writhed as it rearranged itself into a new form.

The wolf that had been Hailey raised its head and howled at the moon.

When my alarm went off, I just lay there for a minute, blinking in the bright sunlight pouring in my window.

Had Hailey ever come back to her room last night? I climbed out of bed and took a peek down the hall. Hailey's door was closed, and I couldn't remember if I had left it open or not.

I tiptoed down the hall and listened at Hailey's door. Nothing. I tapped gently.

The door opened suddenly, and I stumbled backward a step.

"Hi," said Hailey, looking sleepy and confused. "What's up?"

"Where were you last night?" I asked.

"Um . . . here?" she replied, raising one eyebrow quizzically. I'd always wanted to be able to raise one eyebrow.

"I was looking for you, and you weren't here. I listened, but I never heard you come back."

Hailey shrugged. "I was probably in the bathroom,

or downstairs getting a snack. Sometimes I wander around a little at night. I wasn't gone long, though. You must have fallen asleep."

She sounded almost bored, and totally believable. But I noticed a streak of mud on her cheek. And her hair was wild and tangled. *How could she have gotten so dirty in her bedroom?*

"Was there something you wanted?" Hailey asked, self-consciously touching her cheek. I must have been staring at that streak of mud. She looked tired, too, and she had dark circles under her eyes. "Last night, when you were looking for me?"

I forced myself to stop looking at it. "Oh yeah. I wanted to know if you heard the wolf."

"Oh, *yes*." Hailey sighed, and smiled. "Wasn't it wonderful?"

She turned away from me and gently shut her door in my face. I stood and stared at the door blankly for a moment. When she'd turned, I'd seen a dried leaf tangled in her hair; it certainly hadn't been there when she'd said good night. Whatever Hailey said, I was sure she'd spent part of the night outside.

* * *

The scary dream I'd had about Hailey was still bothering me, and I kept remembering everything Anderson had said at school about werewolves. With Hailey's odd behavior the previous night on top of all that, I didn't know what to think. But there was definitely something weird going on.

I found myself watching Hailey carefully over breakfast. She had washed off the mud and combed the leaf out of her hair, but she seemed awfully tired. Molly was making vegan pancakes at the stove, and Hailey sat across from me at the table waiting for them. She leaned forward, elbows on the table, her chin propped on one hand, and gradually her eyes closed and she slumped to one side.

Something touched me on the shoulder.

"Gaaaah!" I screamed, jumping out of my chair and flailing my arms. My hand hit something hard, and there was a crashing noise.

"Marisol!" my mom scolded. When my heart stopped pounding like crazy, I saw her frowning behind me. On the floor was the smashed orange-juice pitcher she must have been holding.

"I'm sorry, I'm sorry," I said. "I'll clean it up. You startled me."

"I guess I *did*," she said, frowning. "That was quite a reaction."

"Sorry," I muttered again. Hailey had opened her eyes and was watching me sleepily but intently, like a cat. Or maybe like a wolf. And I had just seen something I hadn't noticed before: Hailey's ears were pointed.

I got a cloth and helped my mom and Molly clean up the broken pitcher and juice.

"Molly?" I asked, trying my best to sound casual. "I was reading in my room yesterday, um, the werewolf book?"

Molly laughed. "Isn't that a hoot?" she said. "Our guests get a real kick out of it."

"Yeah . . ." I said hesitantly. "This town has an interesting history."

"It certainly does," she said proudly.

My mom smiled. "Anything you want to know about Wolf Valley, Molly can tell you, Marisol," she said. "Her family's been here since the very beginning. Right, Molly?"

"We have," Molly said brightly. "In fact, my family's all mixed up in the werewolf story, if you can believe it."

It felt like my heart stopped for a moment.

"Really?" my mom exclaimed. "You never told me that!"

"Well, it was a long time ago," Molly said. She shook her head a little. "The way this town turned on innocent families was terrible, but it's all in the past."

I slowly turned my eyes toward Hailey. She was ignoring us, twisting a ring on her finger as she stared out the window.

Her ring finger looked awfully long.

The ring was gold, with a turquoise stone set flat into it. A stone in the shape of a howling wolf.

Hailey must have felt me watching her, because she turned away from the window and her eyes met mine. She gave me a long look. Her eyes seemed cool and distant — just like a wolf's eyes in every picture I'd seen. A shiver went up my spine.

Chapter Eight

To: diva12@netmail.com
From: stargirl1013@netmail.com

Tasha:

Weird, weird things are happening here. I can't
really explain, because all the facts seem like
nothing: Hailey has pointed ears, and her ring
finger is as long as her middle finger, and I'm
positive she sneaked out the night the wolf was
howling. Does this make any sense? It was a full
moon, if that helps.

I'm just going to say it, because you're not here,
and I can't say it to anyone who *is* here — I
think Hailey might be a werewolf. Which is crazy.

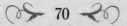

Which is why I can't say it to anyone. Plus I don't want to say it because I feel bad for Hailey, who already doesn't seem to have any friends, and I don't want to make it worse by spreading rumors that she's a werewolf. Tell me I'm insane.

I miss you.
xoxox
Marisol

To: stargirl1013@netmail.com
From: diva12@netmail.com

Hi, Marisol,
You're right, you're insane. Which I warned you was going to happen if you got stuck out in the middle of nowhere, but even *I* didn't expect it to happen so fast.

If you seriously want to figure out if she's a WEREWOLF, the only thing I can tell you (other than to get some mental help ☺), is that I was in a play about a werewolf last summer at theater camp. I can't remember if I told you about it, but

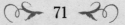

it was called "Full Moon Follies." I played Mira, who was eventually bitten by the werewolf and had to choose whether to become a werewolf or let the mad scientist try out his potion on her. I got to sing a solo and wore this completely fabulous slinky black dress!

Anyway, in the play, werewolves couldn't go anywhere near silver. It was like vampires and crosses — the werewolf couldn't even touch silver without screaming in agony. If we'd had the money for special effects, his hands would have smoked, too. Why don't you get her to touch something silver? Then, after nothing happens, you can forget this.

Or are you just kidding?

Come out of the Valley of Many Mountains, Montana, and call me — I can't tell if you're joking on e-mail.

Miss you!
LYLAS (Love You Like A Sister),
Tasha

Okay. Silver. The idea of werewolves was still a little hard to believe, but I liked to think of myself as a scientist, and that meant I should weigh the evidence and find out all I could before forming an opinion.

I tried looking up "how to tell if someone is a werewolf" on the Internet, but it was really unsatisfying. What I needed was a sensible guide to werewolves in daily life, like *The Idiot's Guide to Werewolf Detection.* But the top results from my search either just listed what Anderson had already told me or were things like "In this Harry Potter book, Snape assigns them a paper on how to identify werewolves" and "In this movie, the vampires can sense werewolves by their smell."

It was like people didn't think werewolves existed in real life. Which they didn't, of course. *Probably.*

That whole day, I kept an eye on Hailey at school. She looked spacey and tired. At lunch, I waved her over to the table where I was sitting with Amber and Bonnie and Lily. Bonnie gave me a funny look, but none of them said anything mean to her. Still, all she did was yawn and smile and say very little. She ate like crazy, though, as if she was totally ravenous. I couldn't help but speculate — had transforming into a werewolf taken a lot out of her?

When I got home that evening, I decided to take action. Tasha's advice was the best thing I had to go on so far, so I rummaged through the little jewelry box I'd brought with me from Austin and found my old charm bracelet. I used to wear it all the time, but it was noisy and got caught on stuff, so I hardly ever wore it anymore.

One of the charms was a silver star, and I slipped it off the bracelet, took a pendant off a necklace chain that was stamped sterling silver, and replaced the pendant with the star.

I went down the hall to Hailey's room and tapped on the door. This time when she opened it, she greeted me with a smile. *We're really starting to become friends,* I thought. What I was about to do would probably make her like me even more (unless she burst into flames), which I felt kind of guilty about. I liked Hailey, but I was partly being nice to her to find out if she was a monster.

"Hi," she said, opening her door wider. "Do you want to see what I'm doing?"

"Sure," I said, and I followed her into her room.

Tons of animals looked out from the pictures on

her walls, but with the lights on, Hailey's room was pretty cozy. The walls themselves (or what I could see of them below the pictures and posters) were painted yellow, and her bedspread was printed with sunflowers. Against one wall there was a desk with another big sunflower painted on the top. Tiny bits of color were spread out across the desk. As I got closer, I realized they were little ceramic squares. In the center was a half-done mosaic made of the tiny squares in a swirling pattern of blue and green.

"Wow," I said. "That's beautiful."

"Thanks," she said softly. "For English, we're supposed to do a response to a poem of our choice, and I thought this would be more fun than something where I had to stand up in front of the class and present. The poem goes: '*Strongly it bears us along in swelling and limitless billows/Nothing before and nothing behind but the sky and the ocean.*' It's by Coleridge. These colors and the circles sort of made me think of the ocean."

"Yeah," I said. They made me think of the ocean, too.

"I haven't been to the ocean yet," Hailey said, "but I'd really like to go. I definitely will sometime. I'd love to see seals in the wild." She grinned at me.

"Um, I have something for you," I said, suddenly feeling shy. "I wanted to thank you for, you know, making me feel welcome here. You've been a star." I handed her the necklace.

"Oh!" said Hailey, surprised and happy. "Thank you!"

She put it around her neck, and when she fumbled with the clasp, I moved forward to help her with it. I don't know what I had been expecting, but she didn't burst into flames or scream in pain. The silver rested around her neck harmlessly.

I returned to my room feeling pretty silly. But still, a little tickle of doubt lay at the back of my mind. The silver test hadn't seemed entirely scientific.

CHAPTER NINE

I was really ready for the weekend. I had just about stopped getting lost in the halls and figured out what was going on in my classes, but it was still hard work.

Saturday morning, Jack came downstairs all lit up and full of energy, bouncing on the balls of his feet.

"Hey there, ladies," he said, tugging my ponytail lightly.

"What's with you?" Hailey asked, amused. "What're you doing up so early on a Saturday?"

"It's a beautiful day," Jack said, sweeping his arm toward the window. "The sun is shining, breezes are blowing, and it's the perfect day to take our new pal" — he pointed at me — "on a ride and picnic."

"Great," I said. It was a little chilly for a picnic, but I'd noticed that people here felt like if there wasn't frost, it was a great day to be outside. "My mom's worried about me riding without an adult, though."

"Don't worry," Jack said. "Hailey and I take new riders out all the time. And there will be three of us, so after you break your leg, one of us can stay with you and the other can go for help."

I stared at him.

"Kidding," he said. "Seriously, my mom knows it'll be fine, and she can convince *your* mom."

And she did. As the only child of a single mom, I'm used to my mom checking everything out for me — she meets my friends' parents before she lets me spend the night at their houses, and she calls to make sure I get where I say I'm going. When I go to visit my dad, it's twice as bad, because he's not used to having me around all the time, so he feels like he needs to be extra careful. But Molly talked and talked about how *responsible* Jack and Hailey were, and how *experienced* on horseback. She said how good they were at teaching new riders, and how they both had first aid certification and had done special overnight horseback trips for years.

Finally, it seemed like my mom was exhausted by all the words, and she agreed to let me go.

Jack led out a brown horse with a black mane and tail and tied it to the fence, then went back to the barn and brought out a black horse and a lighter brown one and tied them next to the first one.

"This is BeeBee," he said, patting the brown horse's neck. "She's very friendly and patient. We always give her to new riders because she's calm and she likes to stay with the other horses — if you don't tell her where to go, she'll come right along anyway."

I stroked BeeBee's nose nervously. She had a white stripe down her face, and the hairs were coarse under my fingers. She blew out air and looked at me in a friendly way.

"She's nice," I said.

"Of course she is," Jack said. He showed me how to use the step to climb up on BeeBee's back and told me how to hold the reins. "This one is Shadow," he said, swinging easily up onto the black horse. "He's my buddy. Hailey usually rides Snowflake here."

"Snowflake?" I said, frowning at the horse. It was undeniably brown.

"I named her when I was six," Hailey called, jogging toward us from the barn. "I'd just seen a TV show with a horse named Snowflake in it. Thanks for saddling her up, Jack. Mom asked me to spray the rosebushes before she beds them down for the winter."

"Hurry it up or we'll leave without you," Jack called jokingly. Hailey sped up, then slowed to a walk as she got near the horses. She reached for Snowflake's bridle, and the horse snorted and stepped quickly back away from her.

"Hey, Snowflake, hey." Hailey followed the horse, making soothing sounds, and it halted, nostrils quivering. When Hailey put out her hand again to take the bridle, Snowflake half-reared, moving backward and shaking her head.

Hailey stopped. "I don't know what's wrong," she said, her voice shaking. "She was fine yesterday. Maybe she's sick?"

"Take Shadow," Jack said, slipping off his horse. "Let me try Snowflake." Snowflake calmed down as Hailey moved away from her, and nuzzled Jack's hand almost apologetically. Hailey reached for Shadow, and he stamped his feet and backed quickly away from her.

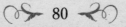

"That's weird," Jack said.

"You *think*?" Hailey snapped. She sounded like she was about to cry. "Snowflake loves me. Forget it. I'll stay home."

Jack frowned. "No, we'll figure this out. Maybe it's the pesticide you just sprayed on the garden. You smell sort of chemical-y. Let me hold Shadow." He took the horse's lead, and patted it on the neck, talking softly. After a minute, Shadow stood still, but when Hailey moved toward him again, he tossed his head and tried to pull away.

"I washed my hands," Hailey said tearfully. "I can still smell the spray, though. If that's what's bothering them, I don't know how to get rid of it."

Jack and Hailey kept trying for a while, but Snowflake and Shadow wouldn't let Hailey get near them, and Hailey was getting more and more upset. The horses stamped and shifted, while BeeBee held still and steady as a rock under me, looking more bored than I'd ever suspected a horse *could* look. I half expected her to pull out a Nintendo DS or something to pass the time.

"Okay," said Jack finally. "Marisol, would you get down?"

"Um," I said, peering down from BeeBee, who

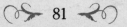

seemed about ten feet high. Was I just supposed to slide off her? Jack held out his hand for me to take hold of it, and I managed to scramble off, although not very gracefully.

"Hailey, you take BeeBee," Jack said. "Whatever's bothering the others, she couldn't care less. Marisol, you can ride Snowflake."

"Yikes," I said. "Remember, I don't know how to ride?"

They both reassured me that Snowflake was a very gentle horse. Hailey wiped her eyes with the back of her hands, and Jack attached a leading rein to Snowflake's bridle. "All you have to do is sit," he said confidently. I wasn't so sure, but eventually found myself up on Snowflake's back. She didn't throw me off, so I guessed I was okay.

When Hailey went to mount BeeBee, the horse showed the most life I'd seen from her, shifting nervously and sidestepping. But she let Hailey get onto her back, and we were off at last.

We took a trail through the woods, and I couldn't help shifting nervously myself. The woods seemed alive with sounds — cracking twigs, chattering squirrels, and branches blowing in the wind. I was uncomfortably aware that, even though Hailey wasn't a werewolf (at least according to the silver test), I had definitely heard *regular* wolves in these woods. And there were probably bears, and maybe mountain lions, too. I like wildlife, but there aren't any big, bloodthirsty animals in downtown Austin.

When we broke out of the woods into a sunny meadow, my worries were temporarily forgotten. The clearing was green and pleasant, and there was a huge snowcapped mountain in front of us. On the mountain, I could see three separate waterfalls. It was gorgeous.

"Nice, right?" said Jack. "Wait until you see what I packed us for lunch."

He'd made soy cheese sandwiches with "special homemade mustard," black bean salad, and, for dessert, double fudge brownies. It was all pretty yummy, though the mustard was definitely unique. The brownies weren't cooked all the way through, but they still tasted delicious and chocolaty.

We were starved after the ride, and we ate and ate, then lay on the picnic blanket, totally stuffed.

"Look," said Hailey, pointing up at a bird circling high above us. "A red-tailed hawk. It's looking for mice."

A little ways off, the horses stamped their feet in the shade. They were restless, and it looked like they were watching us. No, it seemed to me that they were watching Hailey. The silver star hung innocently around her neck.

Was Tasha's idea really a good werewolf test? I couldn't shake the feeling that something was wrong with Hailey and that the horses knew it.

The hawk swooped in lazy circles. I closed my eyes. I wasn't going to think about this now. I was going to bask in the sunshine. My stomach was full, and as the sun warmed me, I felt myself getting sleepier and sleepier.

This time, the sun was shining. As I walked through the woods, I laughed at myself: There was nothing scary here.

Then I heard a rustling and the snaps of breaking wood behind me. Something big was shoving its way through the branches just off the path, and just out of sight.

It was moving fast. I could see branches thrashing as it shoved its way through, but I couldn't see what was making them move.

A low growl split the air.

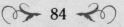

I started to run, suddenly afraid.

It was getting closer, and I knew no matter how fast I ran, it could outrun me.

The growl came again, louder, and closer still.

My heart thumped wildly inside my chest. My hands trembled and my stomach knotted with fear.

Something was coming after me, and I didn't know how to get away. I was absolutely terrified.

CHAPTER TEN

The growl came again, and my eyes snapped open.

My heart was still pounding from the dream.

As it steadied, I realized the growl was thunder. I was lying on the picnic blanket. The sunny sky had turned black with ominous-looking clouds while I slept. I sat up, and a cold wind whipped me in the face; I wrapped my arms around myself and shivered. The horses whinnied and pulled at their ropes.

Jack and Hailey were both napping on the blanket next to me. "Wake up, you guys," I said, shaking Hailey.

She rubbed her eyes and groaned. "Oh, wow, did we fall asleep?" Once she focused, she frowned. "It's going to storm," she said.

Jack had woken up, too, and he looked nervously at the sky. "It's gotten cold," he said, shivering. "We'd better get out of here." They both scrambled to their feet and hurriedly started gathering the stuff from our picnic.

"What's the big deal?" I asked, catching on to their urgency. I scrambled to get the brownie remains into my backpack. "Why are you freaking out? So we get wet."

Hailey fastened the top of her backpack and slung it onto her shoulders. "With the change in the weather, this might be a blizzard. We need to get home fast," she said grimly.

"A *blizzard*?" I said, looking back and forth between her and Jack. "It's *September*. We just had a *picnic*."

Jack shrugged. "It happens. We'd better head back right away."

An icy raindrop hit my face. At the edge of the clearing, the horses were shaking their heads and pawing at the ground.

I'm not going to be able to get on her, I thought, looking at Snowflake. There were no steps out here. But what choice did I have? Jack boosted me up, and somehow I settled into Snowflake's saddle. Jack handed me the reins and was fastening the leading rein to her harness when thunder cracked again, directly overhead.

Snowflake reared, yanking the rein out of Jack's hands. With a surge of speed, she bolted into the woods with me clinging to her back.

We were charging straight toward branches, and I bent low over the horse's neck, trying to shield my face. I wrapped my hands in the reins and hung on to her coarse mane, trying to squeeze her sides with my legs as tightly as I could.

Snowflake was galloping along, and each step was so jarring I felt like I was going to fly right off her back. A pine branch brushed hard against my side, and I closed my eyes. I couldn't get any lower, and I didn't want to see what I was going to hit. I just concentrated on staying on the horse.

Thunder rumbled right overhead. I heard my own ragged panting as the storm broke and the icy rain began to pour down over us. Snowflake tensed and began to gallop even faster. I suddenly pictured her losing her balance on this uneven ground, stepping in a hole, falling, and rolling on top of me.

For a second, I thought maybe I should let go and fall off before that happened. But then I opened my eyes. We were going so *fast*. There was no way I could fall off, even on purpose, without getting really hurt.

I had thought I was holding on as hard as I could, but I forced my cold, wet hands and legs to cling tighter. My clothes were soaked. Something cold and sharp stung my arms and then my face. The rain was turning into hail.

I whimpered as Snowflake lurched, but she caught her balance and ran on. Her sudden swerve made me look to one side, and I thought I saw something gray and yellow. It was gone before I could blink. Had it been one of the elusive wolves of Wolf Valley? Then again, maybe it had just been a ragged bush.

I shrieked as we suddenly burst through a net of thin branches with a sharp cracking noise and found ourselves out in the open again.

There was something big and dark in front of us, and I could feel Snowflake slowing down. Then she stopped and stood calmly.

I took a big gasp of air and started to sob. We were back at the house. Snowflake had run home.

I couldn't move. I just sat there, clinging to Snowflake, shaking and crying as the hail pounded against me. Snowflake shook her head and shifted from side to side, looking back at me as if she was asking why we weren't going to the barn yet.

After a moment, Hailey and Jack galloped into the clearing. The hail had turned to a light, slushy snow.

"Marisol!" Jack called, pulling Shadow to a halt and jumping down to run toward me. "Are you okay?" Hailey dismounted, too, and led the horses toward me.

"I was so scared for you!" she said, her voice shaking. "We didn't know if you would be able to hold on."

I managed to stop crying, but I couldn't talk without starting again, so I just shook my head.

"You're okay," Jack said reassuringly. He held up his hand to help me down. "Take it easy." My fingers were numb, but I managed to untangle myself from the reins and slide off Snowflake's back.

Hailey hugged me. "I'm so sorry," she said. "We shouldn't have given you Snowflake when you can't ride."

I sniffed and hugged her back. "You didn't know it was going to storm. I'm okay."

The door of the house burst open, and my mom,

Mike, and Molly came running out with umbrellas and towels. I let go of Hailey, and my mom wrapped me in a towel, holding me tight.

"Oh, Marisol," she said. "We were so worried when the storm started."

Behind us, Molly was scolding Jack and Hailey for not heading home earlier, and they explained that we had all dozed off. Mike took the bridles off the horses and led them toward the barn. Hailey moved toward him to help, but Snowflake veered away from her, and Hailey stood back.

The horses are still scared of her, I thought.

"Everything's fine now," my mom said, pulling me into the house. But I wasn't so sure.

CHAPTER ELEVEN

The snow didn't last long, and neither did my shakes (although it was going to be a *long* time before I got on a horse again). By Monday, the weather was sunny and I was feeling fine. I had even gone into the stables and fed Snowflake some carrots on Sunday, just to show her there were no hard feelings. "Everyone gets scared," I told her, stroking her long brown nose. *Even me,* I thought, recalling my suspicions about Hailey.

Why had the horses been afraid of her? Had it really just been the smell of the rosebush spray? Had Tasha's silver test worked? What had Molly meant when she said her family was mixed up in the werewolf stories of Wolf Valley? And, most of all,

where had Hailey gone the night of the full moon? I'd tried to ask her about it again Sunday night, but she had just looked me right in the eye and said, "I don't know what you're talking about."

Monday I decided to track down Anderson and see if he knew anything more. This ended up being sort of embarrassing — when I'd asked Amber where his locker was she said, "Why?" and then, with a knowing look, "Oh, I *see*." And then, "Ew. No offense."

"It's not like that," I'd insisted, but she just smiled at me.

I found Anderson at his locker.

"The lovely Marisol," he said, grinning and trying to sound suave. "What's shaking, baby?" He leaned against his locker and spread his arms wide. "Anything I can do for you? My locker is your locker."

"Uh, okay," I said, a little embarrassed. He was *such* a goofball. "Whatever. I wanted to ask you more about werewolves."

His eyes widened and he gave me a big, toothy smile. "You believe me!"

"I'm not sure what I think," I said slowly. "I wanted

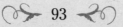

to find out more." Anderson straightened up and got serious. He was clearly flattered that I was coming to him for his expert opinion.

"Well . . ." he began, "they're people who turn into wolves, usually during the full moon."

"I've gotten that far," I said, trying to be patient. "What more do you know?"

He started telling me the same stuff I'd heard from him before, about his great-great-grandmother's neighbor, about long ring fingers and pointed ears. And the fact that, as far as he knew, there had always been stories that there were werewolves around Wolf Valley, but that he didn't know of any real proof. "People would like to prove it," he said. "Lily acts like I'm nuts, but a lot of people around here believe there are werewolves in the woods."

"Have you heard anything about werewolves and silver?" I asked.

"Well," he said, "the traditional way to kill a werewolf is with a silver bullet. Silver is supposed to be a metal that has to do with the moon, so maybe that's why."

"But can werewolves touch silver?" I asked. "They don't burst into flames or feel horrible pain?"

Anderson frowned. "I never heard of that. Are you thinking of vampires and crucifixes?"

"No," I replied, shaking my head. "Do you know of any actual tests to find out if someone is a werewolf? I know vampires don't like garlic, crosses, mirrors, or sunlight, but what about werewolves?"

It would have been easier if I had suspected Hailey was a vampire. There seemed to be a lot of ways to make sure about vampires.

He thought for a moment. "I don't know. I don't think there's anything dramatic like with vampires and crosses. Some cultures say werewolves can't cross running water, but that's a pretty common thing to say about supernatural creatures in general.

"Wait a second," he said, his eyes widening. "Are you asking me this for a reason? Do you think you know a werewolf? Do you have a *suspect*?"

"No, I'm just wondering," I said as I backed away quickly. "Thanks, Anderson. I've got to get to homeroom."

"Seriously," Anderson said, following me a few steps. "Is it Mr. Bonley? Because I've always thought he might be one. He's really aggressive, you know?"

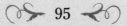

Mr. Bonley was the gym teacher. He was pretty hairy, and really into competitive sports, but I didn't think he was a werewolf. "I told you," I said. "I don't think anyone's a werewolf. I was just curious."

I could have kicked myself. Why had I trusted some play from Tasha's summer camp? One year, they'd done a version of *Romeo and Juliet* set in a spaceship! And Romeo had rapped half his speeches! I definitely had more research to do.

All day I watched for Hailey. I couldn't stop thinking about the possibility that she was a werewolf. Math was the only class we had together, and, as usual, she seemed to be paying no attention at all. She was busy doodling in her notebook. When Mr. Swithin, the teacher, suddenly called on her, I winced in sympathy.

"Hailey, what does x equal in this problem?" he asked.

"Seventeen," she said, without looking up. Her answer was correct.

Wow, I thought. I'd never heard that werewolf powers included mind reading or knowing when you were going to be called on in class, so Hailey was probably just really sharp.

Hailey sat with Amber, Bonnie, Lily, and me at lunch again, and I was happy to see her. Though I was a little freaked out about the idea that she might change into an animal, Hailey had been really sweet to me since the horseback ride. Her being so nice made me feel guilty for thinking bad things about her.

"So is everyone going on the camping trip?" Amber asked as she neatly laid a napkin in her lap and began cutting her mystery meat loaf into eight equal-size pieces. "Of course Lily is."

"Oh, I have to go," Lily said. "And you're coming, right, Marisol? She's the newest member of the astronomy club," she explained to the others.

"I wouldn't miss it," I said eagerly. "I'm really excited. I haven't gotten to use my telescope since I got here."

"Because of the wolves," Bonnie said, nodding.

Hailey snapped to attention. "Wolves?" she asked.

"Yeah, you know," Bonnie said, eyeing her. "The local news always says not to go out alone at night because of the wolf pack around here? They do all those stories about the dangers of wild animals?"

"Oh." Hailey stared down at her lunch. "Yeah. You know, that's really unfair. Wolves aren't aggressive toward humans. Did you know there were less than thirty documented attacks by wolves on humans in the whole twentieth century? And only three of those were fatal, and those were all because of rabies. You're way more likely to get attacked by a dog or a bear, even in areas with a high wolf population."

"It's true," Lily said calmly. "Wolves have a bad reputation they don't deserve."

"Well, but how many people actually go right up to a wolf and don't get attacked?" Amber asked.

"Usually, wolves aren't that close to people, so no one knows. And I think it's still a good idea to stay away from wild animals," Lily replied. Hailey frowned.

"Anyway," Bonnie said, clearly bored with the subject of wolves, "I'm definitely going on the camping trip. It's going to be the most fun thing to happen all fall. Are you coming, Hailey?"

Hailey blushed. "I don't know," she said.

"It'll be totally fun," Bonnie said. "Jack and Marisol are both going. You're not going to sit home alone, are you?"

"I guess not," Hailey said shyly.

"We couldn't do it without Jack," Bonnie said, and she and Amber looked at each other and laughed. It hadn't taken me long to realize that half the girls in school had a crush on Jack.

"Oh yeah," said Hailey, smiling now. "Who else would bring the food?"

"Is it weird for you, having Jack for a brother?" Bonnie asked curiously. "I mean, he's always involved in everything. This school would practically shut down without him. And you're . . . quieter."

Amber flinched a little. We all knew Bonnie hadn't meant it that way, but what she said sounded sort of like: *Jack is an important part of this school. You're not.*

Hailey frowned.

Then she reached up and touched the star necklace around her neck, sighed, and smiled. "It's not weird at all," she said. "Jack's Jack, and I'm me, and we're fine. We're twins, and we're friends, too, but we're different people."

"Absolutely," I said. "And Jack's learning to bake pies, so Hailey and I are two very *lucky* people."

We all laughed, and the awkwardness passed. I added another reason to my list of why I felt guilty about thinking Hailey might be a werewolf: She was clearly making an effort to get along with people (even if, as Jack said, she liked animals better). And I was starting to really like her.

Chapter Twelve

I managed to get my mind off Hailey during our astronomy club meeting. The presentation was on exoplanets, and we made a lot of plans for the camping trip. Lily announced that Jack had promised to get the cooking club to make extra food as well as the hot dogs, hamburgers, and s'mores they had every year.

On the bus home, I started thinking about Hailey again, though. Had I ever seen Hailey cross running water? I kept coming back to her mysterious disappearance the night of the full moon, her dirt-streaked face, and the leaf in her hair the next morning. I also couldn't help but notice her quiet watchfulness, the way she got defensive whenever the subject of wolves came up, and how nervous the horses had

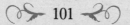

been around her. There were plenty of other possible explanations, I guessed, but it was all so . . . weird. As a scientist, what kind of tests could I do to make sure?

I stared out the window, but all I saw was a blur.

Lily shifted in her seat next to me. "Marisol?" she said. "Earth to Marisol." Her amused tone told me this wasn't the first time she'd said my name.

"Sorry," I said.

"Are you okay?" she asked.

"Yeah," I replied.

"You can tell me if you're worried about something, you know," she said. Her eyes were serious and concerned. "Are you homesick?"

"Not really," I said. Not at all, I realized, a little surprised. I missed Tasha and some of my other friends, but I liked Wolf Valley. My old life seemed a long way away.

I wanted to tell Lily everything. She was smart and practical, and I really wanted someone to talk to.

"Listen," I said, and hesitated. I couldn't tell anyone at school; it wouldn't be fair to Hailey. I was only here for a few months, and Hailey lived here. If I started rumors about her and then left town, I'd be

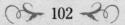

leaving her in a whirlpool of gossip she might be stuck in all the way through school.

"I'm listening, but I'm not hearing anything," Lily joked after a minute.

How could I get Lily's opinion without saying something that would either sound stupid or get her wondering about Hailey?

"Hailey said some interesting stuff about wolves today, don't you think?" I said weakly.

"She was right, you know," Lily said. "Wolves are persecuted by humans in a lot of ways. They're really pretty peaceful animals. For predators. I don't recommend trying to keep one as a pet, though." She grinned and, when I didn't say anything right away, frowned. "Marisol, you're not obsessing about Anderson's crazy ideas, are you?"

"What makes you say that?" I asked guiltily.

Lily sighed and rolled her eyes. "Anderson's got a lot to say, but he's usually wrong. Last year he was sure we were due for a zombie invasion, and had a bunch of kids spending lunch planning how they were going to defend themselves when the zombies arrived. Wolves are interesting, but they're animals. There's no such thing as a werewolf."

*   *   *

Lily's words echoed in my mind as I trudged up the driveway to the house. *There's no such thing as a werewolf.*

Once I got inside, I could smell dinner cooking. The TV was on in the living room, and Molly waved to me from the kitchen. It was all normal and cozy, and I felt a million percent better.

I checked my e-mail. I had told Tasha that the silver test had shown Hailey wasn't a werewolf, and I hadn't shared my doubts with her. Her latest e-mail was full of news about people back home, but for some reason my life in Austin seemed really far away.

On the way to my room, I passed Hailey's open door. The light was on, but her room was empty, and the wall of animals watched me as I peered inside. One gray wolf seemed to be staring right into my eyes, his own yellow eyes wide and his lips drawn back over his teeth in a fierce snarl.

I hurried away, past my room, and tapped on my mother's door. She was sitting at the desk, working on her laptop.

"Hi, honey," she said. "Home already? This day has just shot by. I have so much to do to pull the

November issue together, but I think I may actually finish by deadline." She got up from her chair and stretched. Her curls were messy, as if she'd been running her fingers through her hair all day while she thought.

"Anyway," she said, sitting down on her bed and patting a place next to her, "I'm ready to stop and talk to my girl. How was your day?"

"Pretty good," I said, sitting next to her. "Astronomy club was cool. And we had a science quiz that I think I did okay on." The bed in her room was a sleigh bed, all curving wood, with a big yellow patchwork quilt. The walls were a lighter yellow, with horse pictures hung here and there (Molly said horse pictures were good business for the bed-and-breakfast). It was a happy-feeling room. I traced a square of the quilt with my finger.

"Is something wrong, Marisol?" my mom asked, leaning forward to look into my eyes. "You seem distracted."

I couldn't tell my mom everything. Molly was one of her oldest friends, and we were living in her family's house. But I could tell her some of it.

"Mom, did you ever hear wolves howling outside the house?" I asked.

She frowned. "A few days ago, but not since then. It's nothing to worry about, sweetheart. Wolves stay away from people when they can."

"I'm not worried about the wolves." I said. This was hard. "Well, not because they're wolves. A few days ago, when you heard the howling, there was a full moon, right?"

She looked puzzled. "If you say so."

"Well, there was that book in my room," I said nervously.

My mom's frown disappeared and she started laughing. "The werewolf book? Marisol! That's ridiculous!" She pulled herself together and stopped laughing, although she was still smiling. "Marisol, local legends are good business for bed-and-breakfasts and tourist places. Molly puts those in all the rooms just like the hiking guides. The book's fun to look at, but you can't take it seriously."

"It's not just that," I said hesitantly. "Some of the kids at school say there are werewolves. This one boy told me his great-great-grandmother knew a werewolf. And he said there are more wolves around during a full moon." I couldn't tell her anything about Hailey, but I could mention the creepy feeling I had gotten outside in front of the ranch. "And

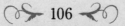

sometimes I have a funny feeling. Like something's *watching* me."

My mother's face was perfectly serious, but her voice still sounded amused. "Listen, sweetheart," she said. "You know my grandmother, my *abuela*, came from Mexico, right?"

"Right." I wondered where she was going with this.

"Well, my *abuela*, God bless her, was a lovely, loving woman, and she used to tell me stories that practically scared the pants off me." My mom laughed, remembering. "There were these great scary, dramatic stories about the *chupacabra*, which is sort of like a vampire, and all kinds of monsters. My dad made her stop for a while because I wouldn't go down into the basement by myself — I was sure *something* was going to jump out at me. But I begged her to start telling them again. Do you know why?"

"Why?" I asked.

"Because I'm like everyone else. People *love* to be scared. And they love telling scary stories. And that's all the werewolves they talk about around here are — stories." She paused. "Maybe you're feeling a bit vulnerable and jittery because you're still getting used to a new place?" I leaned against her and nodded a little. It was true that I was still get-ting used to living here. But my worries about Hailey being a werewolf had *evidence* to back them up. Sort of. I didn't think my evidence would convince my mother, though.

She reached out and stroked my hair, pushing it out of my face. "Does that make sense to you? Does it help?"

"Sure," I lied, and smiled at her.

Really, though? Really, I didn't feel better at all.

Chapter Thirteen

The next week flew by with normal school stuff — homework, gym, quizzes, lunch. And then it was the week of the camping trip. We were leaving after school on Friday, and there was a lot to do. At home, Jack had roped Hailey and me into being his kitchen assistants (Hailey had decided to come on the trip: yay!). And at school, Lily wanted me to go over the millions of details of organizing the trip with her.

Here's what the week looked like.

Monday. During lunch, I met Lily in the science classroom to help her check over the arrangements for the trip. She had checks from everyone who was going, notes on supplies, reservations, and numbers to call. She was going over everything so fiercely that her normally smooth hair had escaped from its

headband, little strands standing up in the air and giving her a wild look.

"Tents," she said to me with a strained intensity. "Sleeping bags. The teachers are driving most people in minivans, and parents are bringing pick-ups with more kids and all the stuff to drop off. We have to remind everyone to bring extra-warm sleep clothes."

"Definitely," I said. It was still light jacket weather during the day, but it was starting to dip down toward freezing at night. "Do you have to plan this all yourself? What about Mr. Samuels?"

Lily shrugged. "He'll check up on what I decide, but I want to get everything right." She tapped a pencil against her desk and went on. "Water. Toilet paper. How much water do thirty people need for a two-night stay?"

"Back up," I said, alarmed. "I thought there were bathrooms and showers and a camp store and things. Isn't this a regular public campsite?"

"Sure," said Lily. "But not in October. After the summer, there's only primitive camping. Everything's closed up. There are pit toilets, but that's it."

I didn't know what a pit toilet was, but I could make a pretty good guess. Yuck.

Lily jumped to her feet. "No!" she said. "Don't look like that! It's going to be *awesome*!"

"Awesome?" I said doubtfully.

"Absolutely," she said, spreading her arms wide and giving me a joyful smile. "Picture it," she went on dreamily, "a starry night, the campfire burning, the smell of wood smoke in the air, the quiet movements of tiny animals, and us, surrounded by the universe."

"Wow," I said, "I never thought about it that way before." I hadn't realized Lily was the type to get poetic about the outdoors. She'd always struck me as very down-to-earth.

"Anyway," she said, and shrugged, "I just want everyone to have a good time."

"We will," I said firmly. *It's only two nights,* I thought. *Who needs running water?* I smiled encouragingly at Lily.

"I'll get online and see if I can figure out how much water the average person needs to use every day," I offered. "Piece of cake."

Tuesday. "Taste this," Jack demanded.

Something smelled good, like roasting nuts. Hailey looked up, keeping her finger in her book to mark her place. "Jack," she said, "we've got a math quiz tomorrow. We don't have time to taste test for you."

"*Taste* it," Jack said again, frowning at his sister. He thrust a spoonful of what looked like grains and nuts at her, and she tried it.

"Not bad," she admitted. "I like the honey."

"What is it?" I asked.

"My special granola," Jack said proudly. "I'm getting ready for the trip. Taste!"

I tried some. It was good. Warm and sweet and chewy. Still . . . "Wouldn't it be easier just to take boxes of cereal?" I asked.

"Cereal from a box is horrible!" Jack said, and then he bared his teeth and actually *growled* at me. For a moment, his face was really scary. His eyes were slits and his hair was bristling.

"Maniac," said Hailey affectionately. Then she turned to look at me.

"Marisol?" she asked, a worried note in her voice. "You look freaked out. Are you okay?"

"Sure," I said. But it had suddenly hit me: *If Hailey is a werewolf, then what is Jack?*

The werewolf book had said whole families were suspected of being werewolves, and that the

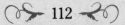

families had disappeared together. They were thought to have retreated to the woods. Was it possible that if Hailey was a werewolf, the rest of her family were, too?

It was hard to picture Molly and Mike as werewolves. And they had definitely been around downstairs, fully human, until late the night of the full moon. So they *must* be human. Plus I figured my mom would have noticed if Molly was a werewolf during the four years they lived together in college. But Molly had said her family was one of those driven from the town for being werewolves, hadn't she?

No, it was a ridiculous idea. Still, though . . . I remembered my friend Olivia back home. Both her parents had dark brown hair and dark eyes, but Olivia was blond and green-eyed. People asked sometimes if she was adopted, but she wasn't — she had inherited her grandmother's coloring. Could being a werewolf be a recessive gene that had skipped Molly?

"Marisol?" Hailey asked again. She and Jack were both staring at me, and I gave them a shaky smile.

"Oh, I'm fine," I said as brightly as I could manage.

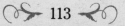

Suddenly, I was very glad we'd be back from the camping trip before the full moon.

Wednesday. After school, I stayed late at the library.

"Can I help you get started?" the librarian asked when I took an unoccupied computer.

"No thanks," I said, "I know what I'm doing." I didn't want anyone to see what I was looking up.

Once she left and I was sure no one was watching, I typed "genetic werewolf" into a search engine. Nothing useful came up.

I typed "becoming a werewolf" and clicked through the most promising-looking links. One was clearly part of a role-playing game, a couple were movie reviews, but one was exactly what I was looking for.

"Ways of Becoming a Werewolf," it said, and it detailed different ways legends said people had become werewolves. It wasn't just getting bitten. If you *wanted* to be a werewolf, you could drink dew from a wolf's footprint (ew), eat a wolf's brain (double ew!), make a magic lotion to rub on yourself (weird), or wear a special flower (lame). You could also become a werewolf by being bitten, or *as the result of a family curse.*

I grinned as I pictured Jack and Hailey mixing up a magic lotion instead of Jack's special granola. But a family curse fit in with Molly's being descended from one of the original families of Wolf Valley. The site also confirmed my thoughts about the fact that becoming a werewolf could be a recessive trait. It said: *Even if you are born into a werewolf family, only some children will inherit the gene, and it may skip multiple generations, only to pop up unexpectedly.*

So Jack and Hailey could be werewolves even if Molly wasn't. She could have carried the gene and passed it down to them unknowingly.

Or Jack didn't have to be a werewolf even if Hailey was: They weren't identical twins, after all. They had different genes. I had to admit to myself that, while I didn't want Hailey to be a werewolf, I *really* didn't want Jack to be one. I pictured his friendly blue eyes, his bright smile — he was just too *sunny* (in the nicest way) to be a creature of the night.

Still, I thought I should probably keep an eye on both of them.

Thursday. Thursday, Hailey and I helped Jack pack his food into coolers, and I was so busy getting ready for the trip I hardly thought about wolves or werewolves at all.

But that night, I dreamed.

I was outside the house in the dark. Everything was calm — I could hear the horses whinnying softly in their stalls, the leaves rustling in a gentle breeze. It was cold, and the stars shone brightly. I could see the wolf constellation, Lupus, right above me.

Nothing was wrong, but I was terrified. I knew something was coming, and then, suddenly, I knew it was there. The normal night noises around me stopped, and there was silence.

I could feel the wolf watching me.

I turned, scanning the trees and bushes around the house, trying to find the animal whose gaze I could feel so clearly. Nothing.

Suddenly, a twig snapped sharply, and I screamed.

I woke up with my mouth dry with terror, my heart pounding. The dream had been pretty bland:

Nothing had actually happened other than a twig snapping, but I had been so terrified, and in the dream I had known why. It was because the wolf was coming, and there was no way I could escape.

Friday. Friday it seemed like hardly anyone could concentrate in class. When the final bell rang, we met in the science lab: twenty-five kids, chaperones, duffel bags, tents, backpacks, coolers of food, water, and sleeping bags.

Anderson was practically vibrating with excitement. He pulled a Frisbee out of his backpack and flung it at random. Someone caught it, and soon it was flying all over the room. "We're going to party in the woods!" he shouted.

I glanced over at Mr. Samuels, who was so deep in conversation with Lily he didn't even notice. But Hailey caught my eye. She was loaded down with a cooler with foil-wrapped packages sitting on top. I made my way through the crowded room to her and took some of the stuff off the top.

"Thanks," she said.

"Should I ask?" I said, nodding to the packages.

"Food, of course," she said. "You should see what

Jack left in the truck." She looked around the room, which was now full of yelling, jumping, and a million different intense conversations. Someone had pulled out a tennis ball and was bouncing it off the wall. "Do you think we'll be going anytime soon?" Hailey asked wistfully. "This stuff is getting awfully heavy."

Surely a werewolf would be super-strong, I thought. One point for Hailey being a regular person. I tried to shake off the thought. Dreams or no dreams, I wasn't going to obsess about it this weekend — I was going to have fun.

Lily hopped up on a chair, stuck two fingers in her mouth, and gave a loud whistle. She reached out and caught the Frisbee, then glared at the boy with the ball until he caught it and stuck it back in his backpack. "Okay," she announced. "Let's hit the road." People cheered and she smiled. "Listen up for your van assignments," she went on, and everyone settled down immediately. I looked at her admiringly. Lily could get a whole group of excited kids to do what she said, without yelling at them.

Assignments were given out, we picked up our bags and tents and everything else, and at last we were off!

Chapter Fourteen

The Two Medicine campsite was pretty, on the edge of a lake, and surrounded by evergreen trees.

We set up the tents and put the food in the storage lockers, which are big metal boxes to keep food safe from animals. Hailey, Lily, Bonnie, and I were sharing one of the four-person tents. It was going to be a tight squeeze: There was really only enough room for four people if everyone was in her sleeping bag. We took turns going in to unroll our sleeping bags and put our backpacks down. When it was my turn, I felt the bottom of the tent. *Yikes*. It was cold and hard, even with the tarp underneath. I was probably going to be tossing and turning and freezing all night. Clearly, I was just a soft city girl at heart.

Once the tents were ready, it was starting to get dark, and Lily and I and the other kids who had brought telescopes began setting them up around the campsite. We weren't going to stargaze until after dinner, when it would be really dark, but we wanted to get ready so we wouldn't have to fiddle with them too much in full darkness.

"Heads up!" came a call behind me, and I flinched as Anderson lurched into me. A second later, his Frisbee bounced off my telescope.

"Hey!" I said indignantly. Bonnie came over and picked up the Frisbee.

"You should be more careful," she said, smiling at Anderson.

"Sorry, ladies," he said. "Sometimes I cannot be contained."

I rolled my eyes and readjusted my telescope as he walked off, but Bonnie smiled and ran her fingers through her red curls. "Do you think he's kind of cute?" she whispered.

I thought about it. There was nothing really wrong with Anderson's looks, but he was so jittery and jokey that I couldn't think of him as cute. "Not really," I said. "Do you?"

She blushed a little and shrugged. "I guess," she said. "I like funny."

The teachers got a campfire going, and soon the smell of cooking hot dogs and burgers wafted over the campground. I wandered over to Lily, who was reading something in her notebook.

"I'm starving," she moaned. "Doesn't it smell good?"

"I'm not really into burgers," I reminded her, "but I am getting hungry. Do you think Jack remembered to bring veggie burgers?"

"Sorry, I forgot," she said. "And yes, I think Jack probably remembered." She gave me a sly little smile.

"What does that mean?" I asked.

"I just think Jack likes you," she said. "He's always looking at you when you're not watching."

Was he? It was a flattering thought, but I shook my head. "Jack likes everybody," I said. "He's just nice to me because I live in his house and our moms are best friends."

"O-*kay*," Lily teased in a singsong voice. "Anything you say."

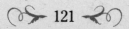

"Is there something in the water here?" I asked. "Bonnie was just telling me she thinks Anderson is cute."

"Really?" said Lily. "Huh. I can see them together, actually. Interesting choice. Now, Jack —"

"Shh!" I said, and I could feel myself turning bright red. Jack was walking toward us holding a plate of food. Lily giggled.

"Hey," he said to us both. "Here, Marisol, I got them to fix yours and Hailey's first so they wouldn't be contaminated with meat grease."

"That was really nice of you," Lily said, nudging me with her foot.

"Thanks, Jack," I said.

"No problem," he answered. "Mr. Samuels cooked the burger, but I brought you some of my secret-recipe coleslaw and potato salad." He nodded encouragingly, waiting for me to take a bite. I took a spoonful of coleslaw and smiled at him. "Mmm," I said. "Good."

"Thanks," he said, looking proud, then turned to Lily. "The meat stuff should be ready now. Come on!" He headed back toward the food.

Lily leaped to her feet and hurried after him. "So hungry," she said, waving at me.

I followed them slowly, looking around. Everyone was getting plates of food, settling into small groups, and talking quietly.

I sat down next to Hailey, and she smiled at me. "Doesn't the fire smell good?" she said. "I love campfires."

"Me too," I said.

Outside the circle of light made by the fire, the forest was dark around us. The light flickered over everyone's faces, and the stars shone brightly overhead. As people finished eating, some of the kids got out their flashlights and left the fire, playing flashlight tag farther away in the clearing.

"Stay out of the woods," Mr. Samuels announced. "We don't want to lose anyone. Remember there are wild animals out there. Put all your food trash and leftovers into the black plastic bags so we can secure them. We don't want to attract bears."

"Or wolves, mountain lions, or coyotes," added Mrs. Abrams, another of our teacher chaperones.

"Yikes," I said, and shivered. I didn't want to think about wild animals roaming outside our tents.

"Don't worry," said Hailey. "I doubt we'll see any animals at all, as noisy as this group's being." She looked wistful.

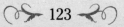

"Time for stargazing," Lily announced when everyone was done eating.

I hurried to my telescope. Bonnie, Amber, Hailey, and Jack joined me, and I showed them Venus, Jupiter, and Mars, and we were even able to see the rings of Saturn.

"This is awesome," said Jack.

"What about the moon?" asked Bonnie. "Let's look at the moon." I focused the telescope on the moon and pointed out the craters. The moon was yellow and almost full, and it hung just above the treetops.

"There's sort of a ring around it," said Hailey. "What is that?"

"It's from the moonlight refracting off ice crystals in the upper atmosphere," I explained. "It's like a rainbow, but from the moon."

"Wow," Hailey said. I glanced over and saw that she was smiling.

After everyone had a chance to look through the telescopes, Lily called us back to the fireside for dessert and storytelling. As I headed over, Jack grabbed my arm and pulled me back behind the others.

"Can I talk to you for a second?" he asked.

I felt a flutter in my stomach. No matter what I said about just being friends with Jack, he was just so cute. Was it true that he liked me? "Sure," I said.

"I've never been able to get Hailey to come along on anything like this before," he said. "She's shy, and people made fun of her last year because she's more interested in animals than people." He hesitated. "Anyway, it's just good that you got her to come."

"Well," I said, and shrugged. "I like Hailey."

"I know," he said. "It's nice." He smiled. "*You're* nice." He squeezed my arm. I felt myself blushing. We stood silently for a moment.

"Anyway," he said, "come on. You have to get one of my special raspberry chocolate brownies before they're gone."

Once we were all sitting around the fire, Lily pointed out some constellations and told the ancient Greek myths behind their names.

Jack was next to me, and I leaned against him just the tiniest bit as I ate my brownie. His arm felt warm and solid, and I couldn't help glancing at him sideways a little. He glanced back at me and smiled, and my insides jumped with a happy nervousness. The fire was crackling. The brownie was delicious. Life was good.

After Lily finished talking, Becka from astronomy club got up.

"Um," she said, twisting her shaggy black hair in her fingers. "This is a true story my brother told me. It happened to some kids he knew when he was our age, right here at this campground.

"These three kids were best friends, and they convinced their parents to let them go camping by themselves. They had a great time, fishing and hiking and cooking over a campfire. But when it got dark, they started hearing weird noises in the woods. They heard branches cracking and leaves rustling. It sounded like something big was making its way toward them through the woods, getting closer and closer. Then they started hearing a terrible groaning noise, like this: *whoo-hoo-hooooooo*.

"One of the guys got scared, and he wanted to call their parents to pick them up. But his friends laughed, and said the noises were just an owl or something.

"He finally got mad and went to bed. He was almost asleep when he heard horrible screaming and banging around, so he ran out of the tent. It was just his friends, yelling and hitting a pot with spoons to scare him. So he went back into the tent and zipped it closed.

"A little later, he was almost asleep when he heard his friends screaming and yelling again and even shaking the tent. He totally wasn't going to fall for it, so he put his head under his pillow and fell asleep.

"The next morning, when he woke up, there was no one else in the tent. His friends weren't in the campsite, but the ground was all torn up around where the fire had been, like something with huge claws had dug at the ground. And when he looked back at the tent, he saw ragged scratches on the sides, as if something with paws as big as his head had tried to claw it open."

Becka lowered her voice and walked closer to us listeners. "They never found his friends. The woods were full of park rangers searching, but they didn't find anything except a few scraps of cloth that might have come from one boy's shirt.

"A year later, the boy who was left behind came back to the campsite. He walked into the woods and he saw something terrible." She paused and looked around at us. I leaned forward to hear. "In the dark of the night...he saw...BOOO!" She suddenly screamed at the top of her lungs.

We all shrieked. I realized I was gripping Jack's arm and giggled. "Sorry," I said sheepishly, letting go. "She scared me!"

"I'll protect you," Jack said mock seriously, patting me on the shoulder.

Everyone was laughing. It was just a joke story: a scary setup to make us jump.

But my eyes went back to the moon, so close to full, and a chill swept over me despite the warmth of the fire.

Chapter Fifteen

It was late when Lily, Bonnie, Hailey, and I crowded into our tent, and I fell into a deep, dreamless sleep right away.

It felt much later when I suddenly opened my eyes onto darkness, wide awake. Something was outside the tent. There was a snuffling noise and a scratching against the tent wall.

"Guys?" I whispered. No one answered. Something brushed against the wall beside my head, and I thought about how thin that tent wall was. *"Guys?"* I repeated anxiously, not whispering this time. I reached out to shake Bonnie, who was next to me.

"Mmmph," she mumbled. "What? It's the middle of the night!"

"So why are you talking?" said Lily sleepily. "Shut up."

"Listen," I said. "There's something outside the tent." There was a pause while they listened.

"There's nothing out there," said Bonnie grumpily. "You're just scared because of Becka's stupid —"

A horrible snuffly growl came from outside, and we all screamed.

"What was that?" Bonnie shrieked.

"You guys?" said Lily suddenly. "Hailey's not here."

My heart plummeted. I couldn't breathe for a minute. I reached out toward where Hailey had been sleeping and found only her empty sleeping bag. Outside, the snuffling noise came again, along with the clattering of something metallic.

Hailey? *But the moon's not full yet,* I thought.

The rest of the campsite was waking up. "What was *that*?" a voice asked, and I heard some boy start making fake, ghostly *ooooooooo*s. "Is it a BEAR?!?" someone shouted.

Lily switched on her flashlight. "I'm going to look outside," she said bravely.

"Yikes," said Bonnie. "If it eats you, can I have your cute black boots?"

Lily made a face at her and unzipped the tent. She stepped outside, and after hesitating for a second, I followed her. Bonnie came after me, hovering nervously in the opening of the tent.

Lily's flashlight beam darted around the campsite. Everything looked normal. The metallic clatter came again, and Lily trained the flashlight beside our tent. "Oh!" she said.

I craned my head to look past her and saw a fat raccoon, its head in an aluminum pan. It was eagerly licking the inside, its little paws holding on to each side of the pan.

Mr. Samuels crawled out of his tent on the other side of the site, a pot in one hand and a spoon in the other. He got to his feet, took a good look at the raccoon, and then started banging on the pot and shouting, "*Aaaaaaaaaaah!* Go! Go!"

The raccoon took its head out of the pan and gave Mr. Samuels a long, offended look. Then it turned and unhurriedly shambled its way into the woods.

By this time, everyone was crawling out of their

tents, laughing and talking and trying to figure out what was going on.

"WHO left food outside of the food locker?" Mr. Samuels shouted accusingly.

There was a scuffling as everyone looked away from the angry teacher. Then Jack slowly raised his hand. "Me, I think," he said. "That looks like the pan the brownies were in. I'm really sorry."

"Next time, don't forget," Mr. Samuels said sternly. "If it had attracted a bear, we would have been in big trouble. Now, everyone, back to bed."

Jack nodded sheepishly, and people started to slowly head back to their tents. I was scanning the campsite. "Where's Hailey?" I whispered to Bonnie and Lily, who looked as anxious as I felt.

Then, behind us, we heard a voice. "What's going on?"

I whipped around to see Hailey, looking cheerful and relaxed. "Why is everyone awake?" she asked innocently.

"Where have you *been*?" I demanded.

Hailey frowned. "I had to go to the bathroom," she said with a shrug. "What's the big deal?"

Bonnie waved her hand dismissively. "Raccoon. Going back to bed." She disappeared into the tent.

Hailey pouted. "I missed a raccoon? I love raccoons! They're so cute."

"Everybody freaked out," Lily said, rolling her eyes. "Good night."

As I settled back to sleep, I smiled. *See?* I told myself. *Everything has a perfectly logical explanation.*

Chapter Sixteen

The next morning, it seemed unusually bright. I groaned and rubbed my eyes. "It's so early," I moaned. "I don't know what time it is, but I can tell it's very early. And cold. Very, *very* cold." When I sat up and my top half came out of my cozy, puffy sleeping bag, it was like I had walked into a giant freezer.

"Up and at 'em," Lily said cheerfully. "It's a beautiful day." She was already fully dressed and busy brushing her hair.

Bonnie grunted, snuggling deeper into her bag. Lily went on, "I've got something to tempt you out of bed." She rummaged in her backpack and pulled out a map. "Today we're going hiking!"

"If you think the promise of hard physical activity is going to get me leaping out of this sleeping bag, you clearly don't know me as well as you think you do," Bonnie said drily.

Lily rolled her eyes and spread the map out neatly on top of her sleeping bag. "Look, there's a whole bunch of trails near us. The guidebook says the best trails for groups are probably the ones to Running Eagle Falls, which is an easy hike, or to Scenic Point, which is a little more challenging."

"Hmm," said Hailey, kneeling next to Lily. "What do you think, Marisol?"

I wriggled out of my sleeping bag and winced as the cold air hit the rest of my body. I had slept in my cozy old sweats, but I was still freezing — I didn't want to think about how cold I would have been in pajamas. I leaned across the tent to look at Lily's map.

The Scenic Point trail clearly involved some serious uphill hiking, and, from the name, probably led to a pretty amazing view. The Running Eagle Falls trail was a lot shorter. I like waterfalls, but I also like hiking, so why not the longer trail? I was about to say so, when I noticed that the Running Eagle Falls trail crossed several winding blue lines. Water. Running water.

I looked at Hailey. She would probably choose

the same hike I did. Silver hadn't bothered her, but that wasn't a real superstition about werewolves, except for silver bullets (and I wasn't going to shoot her). If she could cross running water, would that prove anything?

Not entirely. Something as vague as — what had Anderson said? — *some cultures say a werewolf can't cross running water* — wasn't going to make me stop wondering about Hailey. But if she couldn't cross the water, or if she made an excuse not to cross it, then that would be more evidence that she *was* a werewolf. The experiment was definitely worth a try.

"I think I'll go to Running Eagle Falls," I said firmly, looking straight at Hailey.

"Okay," she said. "Me too."

Lily frowned. "Shoot," she said. "I thought for sure you two would come on the harder trail with me. Bonnie?"

"Are you kidding?" asked Bonnie. "It's either the easy trail or staying at the campground and painting my nails."

"Fine, then," said Lily. "I bet Amber and Becka will come with me."

Bonnie laughed. "Amber will want to jog it."

After breakfast, Amber and Becka did decide to hike to Scenic Point with Lily, along with a few other kids and one of the chaperones. Some of the kids chose to do part of a longer trail, and Jack, Anderson, a bunch of other kids, Mr. Samuels, and one of the other chaperones came with us on the trek to Running Eagle Falls. *Good,* I thought. *I can see if Jack can cross running water, too.*

It had warmed up during breakfast, and it was a beautiful day. The air was clear and fresh. The snow high on the mountain peaks and the scent of the pine trees around us reminded me of Christmas. I realized that when Christmas came in a couple of months, I'd be going back to Austin. For the first time, I felt sad about leaving my friends here and going home.

"Look," said Jack, pointing up at the sky. Overhead, a huge bird circled, looking for prey.

"Is it a hawk?" I said uncertainly.

"A golden eagle," he said. "There are almost three hundred species of birds in the park, and October's still a pretty good time to see them."

"And animals," Hailey added. "Look, there are fox tracks on the side of the trail, and if you watch the mountains, you might see goats."

I scanned the peaks, hoping to see a mountain goat climbing, but didn't see anything. Above us, I could hear squirrels scolding in the trees. Hailey touched my arm and pointed, and I saw a huge white hare hop lazily away from the trail, avoiding us, but not seeming particularly scared.

I could hear rushing water ahead of us and, as we rounded a bend in the trail, saw a rustic wooden bridge crossing a river. *Running water!*

I hung back a little to watch Hailey cross it. Jack strode on ahead of us, but Hailey hesitated. "What's up?" she said. "Did you want to take a picture?"

"Oh . . . yeah," I said. I had forgotten about my camera, but I fished it out of my jacket pocket and snapped a picture of the bridge and the mountain rising behind it.

Hailey stayed standing next to me. I looked at her out of the corner of my eye, trying to tell if she was steeling herself to cross the bridge. "Are you coming?" she asked, a little impatiently.

"Sure," I said, and started walking, trying to be subtle about watching her.

As we walked over the bridge, nothing happened until we were almost across. Then Hailey's foot skidded, and she fell backward.

"Hailey!" I said. "Are you okay?" She was just sitting there. I looked up the path to see if anyone was coming back, but no one had noticed. "Hailey!" I said again.

Hailey pulled herself up, laughing. "What a klutz!" she said. "The wood is wet here."

"You're not hurt?" I asked, and she shook her head.

We walked on over the bridge, my mind buzzing. Had she fallen because of the running water, or had she just slipped? She'd gone over the bridge, but was that even what crossing running water meant? Maybe she couldn't walk through a stream, and crossing a bridge was hard but not impossible.

I was driving myself crazy. It wasn't even like this "not being able to cross water" was a definite thing. I sighed.

We rounded a bend in the trail, and there were the falls. They were amazing, coming from high among the rocks. It was, I saw, actually two falls: a narrow trickle coming down to meet a larger spume of water.

"In the summer, when the water levels are higher, the top falls are stronger and hide the lower falls," Hailey told me. "Some people call it Trick Falls instead of Running Eagle Falls."

Trick Falls. I thought about the waterfall concealed all summer beneath the stronger fall, and how you could see it without realizing there was another level underneath. Was Hailey that way, too? Was the girl who shared her house with me, who rode horses and teased her brother, the real Hailey — but with another, hidden level beneath? Did the full moon reveal Hailey's second level the same way winter revealed the hidden waterfall?

I glanced over at Hailey quietly looking up at the falls. I wasn't sure if I would ever find out the truth about my new friend.

CHAPTER SEVENTEEN

After the hike, I spent the rest of the day hanging out with Hailey, Jack, and my other friends. First, there was a fun scavenger hunt, followed by a picnic dinner and an evening singing songs and making s'mores around the campfire. I was having such a good time it was easy to put my werewolf worries out of my mind.

But once we were in our tent, lying in our sleeping bags in the dark, I started obsessing about it again. I didn't think Hailey was going to bite me or suddenly turn into a wolf, so why couldn't I just let it go? I felt like a little kid again, lying awake in bed, afraid of monsters in the dark.

It took me a long time to doze off, and when I did, my dreams were confused. Quick images flashed

through my mind: *tree branches like skeleton hands against the full moon; the rattle of the wind sweeping through dried leaves; a gleam of teeth.* I didn't sleep well.

In the morning, I felt spacey and anxious.

Bonnie nudged me at breakfast. "Are you okay?"

"Mmm," I said, taking a bite of granola. Hailey was across the clearing, talking to Jack.

"Yeah, I'm just distracted."

She followed my eyes to Hailey and Jack. "Oh, I *see*," she said, giggling.

After lunch, it was time to head back home. I squeezed into the back of a minivan between Lily and Hailey. Bonnie turned around in front of us and whispered to them.

"Marisol *likes* Jack, but she won't admit it."

I could feel myself turning red. Lily looked at Bonnie coolly and shrugged. "Everybody likes Jack," she said. "Isn't that right, Hailey?"

Hailey, straight-faced, nodded. "My brother's very likable."

Bonnie snorted and rolled her eyes. "You know what I mean."

"Seat belts *on*, kids, and face forward," said the teacher driving our van. Bonnie turned back around, flipping her curly red hair over her shoulders.

Lily turned toward me. "So?" she whispered. "Do you?" Hailey raised her eyebrows at me.

I squirmed in my seat. "I don't know," I muttered. "I mean, of course I like him. Like you said . . . everybody likes Jack. What's not to like?"

Lily nodded calmly. "True. And I think he likes you."

"He's my friend," I decided. "I don't know if I *like him* like him, but he's my friend and I like that."

This time, both Lily and Hailey nodded. "Friends are good," Lily said, and smiled.

Hailey said, "He definitely likes you, too. He was saying how cool you are."

"Oh," I said, blushing. "That's nice." Hailey grinned at me and turned toward the window.

We were all quiet for a bit, while the noise of the other kids in the van and the radio playing country music made a comfortable babble around us. On either side of me, Hailey and Lily relaxed, and I saw Hailey's eyes flutter shut as she dozed off.

Like mine, her hair and clothes smelled of wood smoke and pine. I liked Hailey. Couldn't I just let this

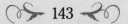

go? Couldn't I just *decide* that there was no such thing as a werewolf and forget about these crazy suspicions?

For some reason, I felt confident Jack wasn't a werewolf. The horses hadn't been afraid of *him* near the full moon. *He* hadn't had any trouble crossing water, and I hadn't seen any evidence that he'd been outside at the full moon either. The only thing that had made me suspect him was that he was Hailey's twin. And I prided myself on being scientific; I knew fraternal twins didn't share all their genes.

But I couldn't seem to get over my suspicions about Hailey. What if she was a werewolf? What could I do about it? The idea of exposing her secret, of people with guns and dogs hunting her down or of doctors and scientists trying to figure out what she was, crossed my mind, and I shivered.

No, I thought, sitting up straight, I could never do that to Hailey. Not to anybody, really, but definitely not to shy, openhearted Hailey, who dreamed of seeing seals in the wild. Never. Even if there was something different about her, I was sure she wasn't a monster.

Could I just let this whole thing go?

I would. I would forget about this crazy idea.

The full moon was coming. It would be here tomorrow night.

It meant nothing. I would forget about the full moon and the wolf howls, and make myself believe that Hailey was an ordinary girl.

CHAPTER EIGHTEEN

The next day, I was totally on edge. By the time my alarm clock went off, I had already been lying awake in bed for an hour, staring at the ceiling and trying to breathe slowly. It was the day of the full moon.

It was easy to tell myself to forget something, but it was much harder to actually do it.

At breakfast, I couldn't help watching Hailey. Her cheeks were flushed, her eyes were glowing, and her hair shone. She looked excited. And that made me nervous.

"Marisol." From the tone of Jack's voice, I could tell it wasn't the first time he'd said my name.

"What?" I asked, making myself turn away from Hailey.

"Pass the milk, please," he said. "Jeez, are you okay? You've been staring blankly across the table for, like, ten minutes."

"Sorry," I said, and passed him the milk. "I'm fine. Just a little tired." Jack was looking at me curiously, and I smiled weakly at him.

"It's a beautiful day," Hailey said cheerfully. "It's the kind of day when it feels good to be alive."

Whenever I saw Hailey during the day, she looked alert and intense. I tried to ignore it, but I couldn't help being aware of her.

At lunch, I was sitting and talking with Amber and Lily when Hailey appeared, smiling.

"Have you seen?" she asked, setting her lunch tray down on the table.

"What?" asked Amber. "I haven't seen anything except today's mystery-meat special."

"Look!" said Hailey, pointing across the cafeteria. We'd been expecting Bonnie to show up eventually — she had gym right before lunch, so she had to change — but there she was, sitting at a table with one other person: Anderson. They were totally focused on each other, smiling and laughing as they gazed into each other's eyes.

"Holy cow," said Amber. "Do you think they're, like . . . a couple?"

"She said she thought he was cute," I remembered aloud. I looked at Bonnie's smile. I couldn't imagine *liking* Anderson — he was so high-strung and hyper — but she looked happy.

"That's Bonnie," said Hailey. "If she wants something, she makes it happen." She nodded. "That's the only thing to do, I've realized. You can't wait around for things to happen *to* you."

Lily looked at her curiously. "Is there something you want to do, Hailey?" she asked.

Hailey shrugged. "I'm just sort of talking about life. You know."

Lily smiled back at her. "I get it."

I wasn't sure I did. Was Hailey acting this way because of the full moon? Bonnie caught us watching her and waved, grimacing at us to stop staring. Hailey drummed her fingers on the table, looking impatient.

"Hey," she said suddenly to Lily and me, "are you two going out with your telescopes tonight? Isn't it a full moon?"

"Um. No," Lily said, a little line appearing between

her eyebrows as she frowned. "Remember, we stay in at the full moon because of the wolves."

Hailey rolled her eyes. "You know," she said stubbornly, "wolves aren't so dangerous. They don't just suddenly attack people."

Lily stared at her. "Wolves *are* dangerous, Hailey. They don't bite people for fun, but it's still not a good idea to get close to them. They're territorial. They're wild animals. They're not *friendly*." She rubbed irritably at the crescent moon–shaped birthmark on her arm.

Hailey rolled her eyes again. The line between Lily's eyebrows got deeper, and she opened her mouth as if she was going to say something, hesitated, then closed it again.

Of course, I thought, *maybe Hailey already knows all about wolves.*

At the after-school astronomy club meeting, Anderson slid into the desk next to mine.

"Pssst," he hissed out of the side of his mouth. "Hey. Psst. Marisol."

"Shhh," I said, listening to the presentation.

He huffed and fished around in his backpack. A minute later, a note landed on my desk:

It's the full moon. 2night. I found out where Bonley lives, and Bonnie and I are going to stake out his apartment. He won't be there if he's a werewolf, but his absence will be a clue. Want to come? Bring something silver just in case.

I had almost forgotten Anderson's suspicion that the gym teacher was a werewolf. I really didn't think he was, but what did I know? As long as he and Bonnie left Hailey alone, Anderson's theories didn't matter. I also really didn't think Bonnie would want me coming along.

"I can't come, but thanks for asking," I whispered. "Let me know what happens. And be careful."

Anderson nodded seriously. "Roger," he said. "Will do."

After astronomy club, Lily and I sat together on the activities bus. She seemed irritable, glaring out at the sun, which was already low on the horizon.

"What were you and Anderson passing notes about?" she asked suddenly. "Did he say anything about Bonnie?"

"Not really," I said. "They're staking out Mr. Bonley's house tonight in case he's a werewolf."

Lily turned and stared at me. "He thinks *Bonley's* a werewolf?" she said roughly. "He's really a nut." This was so different from her earlier, more relaxed view on Anderson's obsessions that I must have looked surprised, because her eyes narrowed. "You don't believe him, do you?" she asked.

"No . . ." I said.

Lily frowned at me. "You sound like you're going to say 'but.' You couldn't possibly think Mr. Bonley's a werewolf. Anderson just hates doing push-ups."

"Well . . ." I hesitated, then leaned closer to her, looking around to make sure no one was listening to us. I wasn't going to do anything about my suspicions, but it might help to talk to Lily. She would never hurt Hailey. "I'm not talking about Mr. Bonley. But there's someone else I'm worried about. There's been weird stuff I've noticed, and it seems crazy, but I can't help worrying" — I took a deep breath — "that she might be a werewolf."

Lily stiffened. "Have you talked to anyone else about this?"

I shook my head. "No, and you can't either. You have to promise not to repeat this, not even to her," I said. "Especially not to her."

"Who are you talking about?" Lily's eyes were wide.

I took a deep breath. "Hailey. I think Hailey might be a werewolf."

"Are you *crazy*?" Lily asked. She shook her head. "Honestly, Marisol, Hailey's been, like, the shyest girl at school forever, and she's finally starting to come out of her shell, and you're calling her a *werewolf*? I thought you were her friend."

"I am her friend," I objected, "but listen —"

Lily put up her hand to stop me. I had never seen her look so angry. "Stop it," she growled. "Marisol, there *are no werewolves*." She whipped around to stare out the window and ignored me for the rest of the ride.

As the bus stopped to let me off, I got to my feet and then paused next to our seat. "I'm sorry, Lily," I said softly. She didn't answer.

Great. Now Lily was mad at me. I sighed. I should

have kept my thoughts to myself. I climbed off the bus and headed toward the house. Jack had gone to a friend's after cooking club, and I was sorry he wasn't there. I could have used a friend to take my mind off Hailey.

Chapter Nineteen

During dinner, Hailey was restless. Her glass chimed as she tapped her fingers against it, and her plate jumped as she beat out a rhythm on it with her fork. Jack raised his eyebrows at her across the table and whispered, "Hail, what's up with you?" to which she just shrugged. Our parents didn't seem to notice a thing.

"A toast!" called out Mike cheerfully. "Here's to a month of living together. I know I speak for Molly and the kids when I say we couldn't have enjoyed it more. You know you're welcome to stay as long as you like," he added, smiling.

"Hear, hear," said my mom, tapping her glass against his. "I just want to say how much Marisol and I appreciate the way you've opened your home and your family to us."

We all touched glasses. Jack smiled as he tapped his water glass against mine. It seemed like we were in a golden glow of friendship. But I couldn't stop thinking about how, outdoors, the sun was setting and darkness was beginning to fall. I wanted to run outside of that warm golden glow and see if the moon was rising.

After dinner was over, Hailey cleared the table and kissed her parents. "I'm going to read for a while," she said sweetly. "I'll probably go to bed early, so I'll say good night now."

I looked at the clock. It was seven thirty.

Didn't anyone else think it was weird that Hailey was going upstairs to bed so early?

I guess not, because her parents and my mom just smiled and said good night. Jack waved a hand to her as he slouched off into the living room to watch TV.

"I'm going to go up, too," I said quickly. "I have more homework to do, and then I'll turn in." There was no way Hailey was a werewolf. But still . . . just in case . . .

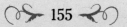

I hurried up the stairs after her.

When I got to the second floor, Hailey was going into the bathroom, so I went into my room to read. I couldn't focus. All my senses were on edge, wondering what she was going to do. After I heard her go into her own room, I waited another half hour, watching the clock, then went after her. Just to check.

I knew she wasn't going to be there.

I tapped on her bedroom door.

"What?" she said.

Oh.

I opened her door. Hailey was curled up on her bed with a book.

"Nothing," I said. "I mean . . . have you seen my red sweater?"

She shook her head.

"Okay," I said awkwardly. "Thanks."

I went back to my room. *See?* I told myself. *She's just lying there reading, like she said she was going to. She's not sprouting fangs or sneaking out to howl at the moon. Now let this go!*

Twenty minutes later, I headed down the hall. Maybe it would be easier for me to concentrate on my homework if I was in the same room as Hailey. I

hoped she wouldn't mind a reading buddy. I tapped on her door. No one answered.

I opened the door. The light was still on and Hailey's book lay on her pillow, but Hailey was gone.

CHAPTER TWENTY

The white curtains at Hailey's window billowed in with the breeze. I felt frozen. I had more than half expected to find her still in her room. I walked over to the window and looked out.

The branches of a big tree reached almost to the window, and the sloping roof would provide some support if someone wanted to climb across the branch and into the tree. Is that what Hailey had done? I looked down and shivered. In the dark, I couldn't even see the ground beneath the window.

No way. I wasn't even going to try going out that way. I left Hailey's room and stealthily tiptoed downstairs, pausing at the bottom of the stairs to listen. I could hear the TV in the den, so Jack was still in there, and then I heard Mike's voice and knew he

had joined Jack. My mother and Molly were talking in the kitchen.

I slid through the hall, holding my breath as I passed the entry to the kitchen, and quickly and quietly undid the lock on the front door. I slipped outside and closed the door softly behind me.

Outside, I started shivering immediately. I should have brought my jacket. I wrapped my arms around myself and ducked my head against the wind. It was dark and the air smelled like frost. The wind kicked up, rustling dry leaves against the house. The full moon shone above me, lighting up the woods around the house. I could hear the horses whinnying rest-lessly in their stable.

This was stupid. If Hailey was even out here, how was I going to find her? She could have gone anywhere after she climbed out her window. I started working my way around the house, heading away from the stables, skirting flower beds and bushes.

When I reached the back of the house, I looked up at Hailey's open window. It glowed golden in the darkness, throwing a long rectangle of light on the ground. I bent over to inspect the earth around the bottom of the tree. I was hoping to find

footprints — or paw prints — but the ground was hard and, if there was anything to see, I couldn't find it. I should have brought a jacket *and* a flashlight.

I gazed out into the dark of the forest. If there was anything out there, how was I going to be able to see it? I realized that I should have stayed closer to Hailey, so that I could have followed her when she left the house.

I was just wondering if I should give up and go back inside when I saw the light. It looked like the thin beam of a flashlight in the woods.

I hurried toward it.

The full moon was overhead, and twigs cracked under my feet. I was cold and scared and suddenly reminded of my dreams. Was I about to meet a were-wolf in the wild? What would I do? I was getting close to the beam of light, and I slowed down. Was I in danger? What would a werewolf be doing with a flashlight anyway?

I blundered toward the light, branches catching at my clothes. Suddenly, the light was in my eyes.

"Marisol?" I heard Hailey ask in a confused, and definitely human, voice. She turned the light aside so it wasn't shining right in my eyes. "What are you doing out here?"

"What am *I* doing out here?" I said. "What are *you* doing out here? I came to find you!"

"Oh no!" Hailey said. "Did my parents realize I went out? Is everybody looking for me? I'm in so much trouble!"

"No," I reassured her. "I'm the only one who knows you're out here. Unless they've realized since I left that we're gone, and then we're both in trouble."

I reached out and took the flashlight and turned it on her. Hailey looked bright-eyed and excited, but completely normal. I noticed *she* had been smart enough to put on a coat and hat, so she looked a lot warmer than I was. Her blond hair was springing out from under the hat, but it wasn't turning into fur. The full moon was high in the sky above her, and it was definitely, absolutely, clear that Hailey was not a werewolf.

That was a relief.

I suddenly felt really stupid.

"Hailey," I asked again, "why are you out here? Did you come out here last month? I noticed you were missing then."

"Yeah," Hailey said. She sighed. "I really want to see a wolf in the wild. You know they're spotted around here a lot more during full moons, right? And there are all kinds of stories about them: that they have special powers, or even that they're were-wolves. But I haven't had any luck. Last full moon, I climbed a tree and stayed in it almost all night, wait-ing for the wolves. I fell asleep and nearly fell out of the tree. I barely woke up in time to catch my balance."

Just then a wolf howl shattered the quiet of the night.

Hailey grabbed my hand. "Did you hear that?" she asked. She was shaking with excitement.

I was shaking with fear. "Hailey," I said, "we need to go back to the house."

"Are you kidding?" she said. "It sounded so close!"

"Exactly," I said. I turned off the flashlight. Maybe the wolf wouldn't be able to find us in the dark.

No, that was ridiculous. And didn't wolves avoid people when they could, anyway? I turned the flash-light back on. "Hailey, wolves might not attack people all the time, but that doesn't mean they won't if they feel threatened, like if two kids jump out at them in the middle of the night."

Hailey stood still for a minute. "I guess you're right," she said finally. "But I really . . . I've always wanted to see a wolf for real." She sounded close to tears.

"We'll go to the zoo," I told her. "It won't be the same, but it'll be pretty good, and a lot safer. And we'll make a donation to a save-the-wolves charity. Just *come on.*" I was listening for another wolf howl. That one had sounded awfully close, but which direction had it come from? Were we safe to head back the way I'd come? If not, maybe we'd have time to climb a tree, like Hailey had last month. I yanked Hailey's arm. Slowly, she started to move after me.

Then we froze.

There was a wolf blocking the path out of the clearing.

"Oh my gosh," whispered Hailey. She sounded half-thrilled and half-terrified.

It was thin and gray with touches of brown on its ears and legs. It looked young, small, and skinny. Its ears tipped forward, and it looked from Hailey to me and whined sharply. Its golden eyes were fixed on us almost as if it was trying to tell us something, and it slowly moved closer to us.

Another howl rang out in the distance.

I held on to Hailey's arm tightly and backed slowly away from the wolf, pulling her with me. The flashlight shook in my hand, and the beam skittered around the clearing.

The wolf stopped and stared at me again, whining softly. I steadied the flashlight. It panted, tongue out, and, as the flashlight beam settled on it, I noticed a dark, golden, crescent moon–shaped mark on one of its front legs.

That moon . . .

I stared into the wolf's eyes. Was there something familiar there?

"Lily?" I breathed.

CHAPTER TWENTY-ONE

"Lily?" Hailey echoed. "Marisol, you don't think . . . Lily can't be a wolf."

I was suddenly absolutely sure. There was a wolf in front of me, but I knew that it was my friend Lily. It wasn't just the crescent moon mark on its leg that matched Lily's birthmark, or the expression in its eyes that, now that I looked, seemed so familiar. The way the wolf stood, watching us, reminded me of Lily's steady calm.

"Wow," I said. "No wonder she didn't want me talking about werewolves."

The wolf pulled its lips back over its — her — pointed teeth as if she was smiling, agreeing with me. Or snarling, warning me.

Another howl in the distance, closer this time.

The wolf bounded toward me and I flinched. She grabbed the hem of my jeans gently in her teeth, without touching my skin, and began tugging me back toward the house.

"Hailey!" I shouted, panicking. Lily tugged harder on my pant leg. A second wolf's howl answered the first. They were coming closer.

"I think we'd better go, Marisol," Hailey said, her voice shaking. "I think we should do what she wants."

Lily dropped my pant leg and pushed her head against me hard. Then she shoved Hailey with her shoulder, pushing her back toward the house.

"Come on!" Hailey said, and started to run.

I glanced back into the woods. Were yellow eyes watching me from the darkness? Wolf-Lily, standing next to me, growled and pushed me again, then took off running, her long lope quickly taking her out of the clearing. I ran after her.

Branches hit my arms and face, and I dropped the flashlight. I didn't stop to pick it up. I stumbled and tripped over rocks and branches. Ahead of me, I could hear Hailey's pounding feet as she ran. There was a thud as she fell, and I almost tripped over her.

"Come on!" I said, pulling her up. "Come on!"

We were both gasping for breath and staggering now. We held on to each other as we got close to the house. More howls erupted behind us. Were they on our trail?

Suddenly, we were by the house again. The lights were still lit downstairs, and I fumbled for the doorknob, trying to be fast and quiet.

"Marisol," said Hailey softly beside me. She was staring out of the little circle of light cast by the house's windows. I followed her eyes.

In the shadows just outside the light stood the wolf. Lily? She growled softly and twitched her ears in an impatient way, as if saying, *What are you waiting for? Get inside now.*

Instead, Hailey walked toward her.

"Hailey," I said warningly. I was sure it was Lily and that she was helping us, but still, I didn't know how much of her was just Lily right now and how much was the wolf. I didn't think it was a good idea to get too close to her if we could help it.

Hailey kept going until she reached Lily, then knelt on the ground in front of her.

"Lily?" Hailey said hesitantly, and held out her hand like she might to a dog. "Lily, thank you," she said.

The wolf sniffed her hand briefly, straight-legged and dignified, and then, very briefly, dipped her head before turning and disappearing, quickly and silently, back into the forest.

"Wow," said Hailey a few minutes later. "Just wow." She shook her head. "I can't believe this."

We had managed to slip back into the house and upstairs without anyone seeing us. I had half expected our parents to be either out searching for us or waiting by the door to ground us forever. But everything was quiet. Hailey and I were sitting on her bed, still totally shocked.

"I never would have guessed," said Hailey, shaking her head again. "And *Lily*. Wow, I mean, Lily is, like, the most normal person I know."

I thought for a long time before I said anything. "Listen, Hailey," I said finally. "We can't tell anyone about this."

She looked at me seriously. "I know," she said. "We can't. And who would believe us, anyway?"

"Well . . ." I paused. "Anderson would. He's staking out the gym teacher's house right now to see if he turns into a monster."

Hailey giggled. "Anderson. Did I ever tell you about how in fourth grade he convinced me I had psychic powers? He had a bunch of us trying to start campfires with our minds. He'll believe anything."

"I know." I laughed.

Hailey sat up straight. "Can you imagine how Lily must be feeling, though? We have to do something."

"Like what?" I said. "Make her an 'it's okay you're a werewolf' card? Take an oath of silence?"

Hailey shrugged. "She probably is hoping we don't really know."

A drawn-out howl rose outside in the distance. I shivered. "Do you think that's her?"

Hailey sighed. "Do you know what?" she asked. "I think it must be really lonely to have such a big secret."

I nodded and leaned back against the wall behind Hailey's bed. Outside, the full moon sailed high in the sky. I thought about Lily: smart, capable, scientific Lily, and the huge secret she was keeping. I felt so sad for her. I had Tasha, and now Hailey, but how could Lily ever really be close to anyone? She had to keep so much of herself hidden. Could Hailey and I help her, now that we knew the truth?

Chapter Twenty-two

The next day, even though it seemed like the world had changed forever, we still had to get up and go to school. Hailey looked as sleepy as I felt over breakfast, and we barely spoke at the bus stop or on the bus.

"What's the matter with you?" Jack finally asked, exasperated, as we headed for the front doors of the school. He'd been trying to talk to us about school, the TV show he'd watched the night before, cooking, and all sorts of stuff, and Hailey and I had hardly spoken a word.

"Sorry," I said, blushing. "I guess we're both tired." Hailey nodded in agreement.

Jack looked at us suspiciously, then shrugged.

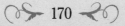

"Okay," he said. Jack wasn't nosy, and I added that to my mental list of things I liked about him.

All morning, I looked for Lily. I kept thinking I had seen her, but it would be just a flash of honey-colored hair as someone whipped around a corner, or a glimpse of a straight-backed figure walking quickly along in a crowd.

"Have you seen Lily?" I asked Bonnie when I ran into her near my locker.

"Uh-uh," she said casually, fiddling with her bracelet. "What about her?"

"Um," I said, "I guess I'm just looking for her. I haven't seen her today."

"Mmmm," Bonnie said. "I'll tell her if I see her." She brightened. "Marisol, I had the most amazing time last night."

"Yeah?" I asked, interested despite everything else that was going on. "With Anderson?"

Her eyes widened. "I only went with him because he's cute when he gets all excited about something, but I think he might be right about Mr. Bonley," she said. "Bonley's house is dark and spooky, and he went out really early and didn't come back before we had to go. We walked around the building, and there were these weird paw prints, like a big dog's, in the backyard, and we think they might be a wolf's."

I wanted to ask if she was sure Mr. Bonley didn't just have a pet dog, and then I remembered the howling in the woods last night and changed my mind. I knew now that Lily was a werewolf, and it seemed pretty unlikely that she was the only one. Who was I to say Mr. Bonley wasn't one, too? It was a scary thought, because Lily had definitely been afraid for us last night. And when a wolf is scared, there's something to be seriously scared of. Maybe the other werewolves weren't so gentle.

"Just be careful," I said to Bonnie. "If you guys are right, he might be dangerous, especially with a secret like that."

She nodded seriously. "Yeah. And even if he's not a werewolf, he's kind of a mean gym teacher," she said. "I don't want to get caught sneaking around his backyard. He'd probably make me do twice as many push-ups in gym class for the rest of my days in middle school!" She grinned. "Don't worry — I can keep Anderson under control."

By noon, I was sure Lily was avoiding me. I wondered whether I'd see her at lunch. But when I entered the cafeteria, Lily was sitting at our regular table with Amber. She sat up straighter when she saw Hailey and me come into the cafeteria. She looked brave and wary, like a soldier in enemy territory.

"Hi," we all said, and there was a little pause.

Then Amber tightened her ponytail and said, "I don't know if you guys have been thinking about the student council bake sale at all, but we're raising money for a winter dance. The student council is asking everyone to bake goodies for it and, of course, to buy stuff. Jack's making brownies, but can you cook, Marisol? Or you, Hailey? The more the better."

"She knows I set fires trying to make toast," said Lily, giving a strained-looking smile. "But I promise to buy at least three things."

Amber frowned. "Lily, that's not funny. You could have burned down your house." She got out her notebook and looked at me expectantly. "Is there some kind of Texas thing you could make?"

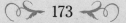

As we talked about the bake sale, things felt easier. I had to promise to make cactus-shaped cookies, and I also had to convince Amber that Texas toast was just garlic bread and not a regional treat everyone would love to try.

Just as I was relaxing, Amber zipped her notebook and pen back into her backpack.

"Where are you going?" asked Lily anxiously.

"I've got a field hockey meeting," Amber said. "We're going to watch the tapes from our last game and talk strategy. See you later."

After she left, we sat in silence for a while. Then Hailey cleared her throat. "So . . ." she said, "how was your night?"

"Fine," said Lily tightly.

"Yeah," said Hailey. "It was very quiet for us. I went to bed early and slept like a rock." She looked at me meaningfully. "How about you, Marisol?"

I caught on. "Me too," I said. "I don't even remember dreaming."

Lily looked down at her lap. "Uh-huh," she said.

"I do wonder, though," Hailey said casually. "You know, Anderson's been talking about werewolves a lot. He thinks Mr. Bonley is one. What do you think?"

Lily hesitated. "There's no such thing as were-wolves," she said determinedly, then her face softened a little. "If there were, though, I bet they'd be just a couple of families. Maybe people who have been here a long time and who want to be left alone."

"Oh," I said. "So you don't think people get to be werewolves by getting bitten, or by maybe drinking water out of a wolf's paw print?"

They both stared at me for a minute, then giggled. Lily shook her head. "Probably not." She sighed. "I would think, though, that it would be a secret that people would do anything to protect. It might not be safe for other people to know about it."

Hailey and I nodded in agreement.

"Right," said Hailey. "You know, I used to go out at night looking for wolves, but I don't want to anymore." She looked seriously into Lily's eyes. "Lily?" she said. "You know, my family's lived here a long time."

Lily raised her eyebrows. "Mine too."

"Well, I've always been ashamed of some of the things my ancestors did. They, um . . . treated other people unfairly. The stories about that made me think people were a lot worse than animals." Hailey

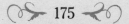

hesitated. "I've always wanted to make it better somehow."

I thought of the townspeople who had driven out their neighbors. Molly had said her family had been part of that story, but she hadn't said which part. I'd gotten it wrong — they hadn't been the werewolves, but the frightened people who'd burned down their neighbors' houses and chased them out of town.

Lily and Hailey exchanged a long look. "Sometimes, having friends who support you is a big deal," Lily said.

"You know, on a totally unrelated note, I wanted to tell you both that, even though I haven't been here that long, I feel like we've become really good friends," I added. "And if one of my friends ever happened to have a secret, I would never, ever tell anyone."

"Me neither," said Hailey. "That's how friends are."

Lily looked up and gave us a weak smile. Her eyes were glistening, and she looked like she might start to cry.

"On the other hand," said Hailey casually, "if a friend wanted to talk about *anything*, I think it's really important to listen. And not to repeat anything, ever."

"I think that's so true," I agreed.

Lily's mouth trembled. "Just generally speaking, it can be good to talk," she said in a soft voice. "My family can be tough to talk to about some things." She hesitated. "They have a particular point of view that's maybe a little different than the point of view a friend might have. If you see what I mean."

Then she gave us a real smile, and Hailey and I smiled back. It was like we were in this warm little circle of friendship and secrets just between the three of us. I thought about each of them, and about Bonnie and Amber, and Jack, too, and horses and mountains and the big Montana sky overhead.

Hailey sighed. "I'm going to miss you, Marisol," she said. "Things have changed a lot for me since you've been here."

"Yeah," said Lily. "I feel like we've just started really being friends."

I cleared my throat. My mom and I had been talking about whether we should extend our stay, and I'd been going back and forth: I missed home, but I really loved Wolf Valley, too. And I felt so close to Hailey and Lily after our adventure the previous night. "You know," I said, "my mom would stay the rest of the school year if I wanted to."

"Really?" said Lily.

"My parents are dying for you guys to stay," Hailey said. "Me and Jack, too."

I grinned at my new friends. "It's only October," I said. "I can't wait to see what happens in this town the rest of the year."

I would have to explain to Tasha and reassure her that she'd always be my best friend, even if she didn't see me until summer. I knew she'd miss me, and I'd miss her, too.

But I was just starting to understand life in Wolf Valley. As a scientist, I was sure there was a lot more to find out about this little town. My mom had been right: So far, my time in Montana had been a great adventure, and I had a feeling it wasn't over just yet!

BITE INTO THE NEXT POISON APPLE,
IF YOU DARE. . . .

The room was dark. "Um, hello?" Anna said.

"Come in," said a voice from somewhere in the darkness. "Close the door."

Anna and Dory stepped inside and let the door swing shut behind them. Because there were no windows, the room was almost completely black. The only light came from a crack under the door.

Anna gave a little yelp as a light came on, illuminating a frightening face. It took her a second to realize it was Jessamyn. She was standing against the far wall, holding a flashlight under her chin to light up her face in a spooky way. Anna could see two figures standing on either side of her. Kima and Lauren.

"Welcome," said Jessamyn. Suddenly, she swung the beam onto Dory's face like a spotlight. "What's she doing here?" she asked Anna sharply.

"She — she's my friend. I told her she could come," Anna stuttered.

One of the other girls — Lauren, Anna thought — stepped forward. "She's not supposed to be here —"

Jessamyn cut her off. "That's all right. The more the merrier." Anna thought she heard a smile in her voice. But at once, she became serious again. Swinging the flashlight beam onto Anna, she asked, "Do you know why you're here?"

The light was blinding. Anna held up a hand to shield her eyes. "The note. It said I was chosen. . . ."

"That's right," said Jessamyn. "You have been specially chosen by me to be part of a secret club. Do you accept?"

Anna was about to say yes, but before she could, Dory broke in. "What is the club, exactly?"

There was a pause, as if Jessamyn was deciding how to answer. "I can't tell you. All the members are sworn to secrecy. You have to join first. Are you in or are you out?"

"In," Anna said promptly. She nudged Dory, who, after a moment's hesitation echoed, "In."

"Good." Jessamyn nodded. "But first you must go through the initiation."

"Initiation?" Anna asked with a shiver. All the darkness and secrecy were starting to get to her. Why couldn't they just turn on the lights?

Kima spoke up. "To be in the club, you must pass a test. You must face the spirits."

"How do you do that?" Anna's voice came out in a squeak.

"You have to look into the mirror and call on them," Lauren said. "If they say so, you can be in the club." She paused then added dramatically, "But if they don't like you, they could kill you."

Anna gulped so loudly she was sure everyone in the room had heard.

"This is stupid!" Dory suddenly burst out.

Anna turned to her friend with a gasp. *Shut up,*

Dory! she thought in horror. She was going to ruin everything!

Jessamyn swung the flashlight beam onto Dory, who blinked in the sudden light. "Are you afraid?" she asked coolly.

"No," Dory snapped. "I think you're playing some dumb game, and I'm not interested. Come on, Anna." She turned to leave.

But Anna didn't move. Hadn't she been longing for something like this — something exciting, something to set her apart from the rest of the kids at Wilson? She wasn't willing to give it up so quickly.

Dory made a noise of disbelief or frustration, Anna couldn't tell which. They heard her stumble as she groped for the door. Then it swung open and closed, and Dory was gone.

"Sure you don't want to follow your lame friend?" Jessamyn asked Anna.

"No," said Anna. "I'm ready."

Jessamyn led her over to the mirror and handed her the flashlight. She showed her how to hold it under her chin. Held at that angle, light carved Anna's face with eerie shadows.

"Now, look into the mirror and say, 'Spirit in the mirror, I call on thee, come tell us what is to be.'"

"Spirit in the mirror, I call on thee . . ." Anna repeated. Her voice sounded high and uncertain. Behind her, she heard someone snicker.

Suddenly, Anna felt a flicker of doubt. What if Dory was right? Was this all a game, just some big joke?

"Don't stop!" Jessamyn commanded. "Look into the mirror. Keep repeating it."

"Come tell us what is to be." Anna sensed movement in the darkness behind her. What were they *doing*?

She didn't have time to wonder . . . because something was happening in the mirror. Her reflection was *changing*.

A face was emerging from the mirror's depths, like a swimmer surfacing through water. Little by little, its features took shape. Anna's heart gave a leap of joyful recognition, followed by a stab of fear.

The flashlight fell from her hand. Anna swayed, clutching the edge of the sink for balance as the room swung around her.

Distantly, as if from miles away, she heard Lauren say, "Look at her. What's *wrong* with her?" Then everything went black.

candy
APPLE

read
them all!

Life, Starring Me!

Callie for President

Drama Queen

I've Got a Secret

Confessions of a Bitter
Secret Santa

Super Sweet 13

The Boy Next Door

The Sister Switch

Snowfall Surprise

Rumor Has It

The Sweetheart Deal

The Accidental
Cheerleader

The Babysitting Wars

Star-Crossed

Accidentally
Fabulous

Accidentally
Famous

Accidentally
Fooled

Accidentally
Friends

How to Be a Girly Girl in
Just Ten Days

Ice Dreams

Juicy Gossip

Making Waves

Miss Popularity

Miss Popularity
Goes Camping

Miss Popularity
and the Best Friend Disaster

Totally Crushed

Wish You Were Here,
Liza

See You Soon,
Samantha

Miss You, Mina

Winner Takes All

POISON APPLE BOOKS

The Dead End

This Totally Bites!

Miss Fortune

Now You See Me...

Midnight Howl

Her Evil Twin

THRILLING. BONE-CHILLING. THESE BOOKS HAVE BITE!